Sally's Story

Aideen Walsh

Copyright © 2024 Aideen Walsh

All rights reserved.

ISBN: 9798876720016

DEDICATION

To my husband, Larry, our four children and their spouses; last but by no means least, our nine wonderful grandchildren.

CONTENTS

DEDICATION iii
CONTENTS v
ACKNOWLEDGMENTS i
Chapter One 1
Chapter Two 5
Chapter Three 11
Chapter Four 15
Chapter Five 20
Chapter Six 24
Chapter SeveN 30
Chapter Eight 35
Chapter Nine 40
Chapter Ten 45
Chapter Eleven 51
Chapter Twelve 55
Chapter Thirteen 59
Chapter Fourteen 63
Chapter Fifteen 68
Chapter Sixteen 72
Chapter Seventeen 76
Chapter Eighteen 81
Chapter Nineteen 86
Chapter Twenty 92
Chapter Twenty-One 97
Chapter Twenty-Two 101

Chapter Twenty-Three 107
Chapter Twenty-Four 111
Chapter Twenty-Five 117
Chapter Twenty-Six 123
Chapter Twenty-Seven 127
Chapter Twenty-Eight 132
Chapter Twenty-Nine 138
Chapter Thirty 141
Chapter Thirty-One 144
Chapter Thirty-Two 148
Chapter Thirty-Three 154
Chapter Thirty-Four 159
Chapter Thirty-Five 163
Chapter Thirty-Six 167
Chapter Thirty-Seven 171
Chapter Thirty-Eight 175
The Escape Route Series 180
ABOUT THE AUTHOR 181

ACKNOWLEDGMENTS

As always, I could not have done this without the feedback received from my critique partners, particularly Diane. A big thank you to my beta readers and especially Jen and my daughter-in-law, Rachael, who can always be counted on to read and respond.

CHAPTER ONE

Just when I thought I was going to scream from the pain, the server approached our table and asked Malcolm if we needed anything else. He immediately lifted the fork he'd been pressing into my thumb and asked for another beer and the check. I headed for the restroom. Thankfully, it was empty. As I held my throbbing hand under the cold water, a woman came in. She stood beside me; her concerned look reflected in the mirror. I could feel myself blushing as I looked away. She wasn't much taller than five feet, at least six inches shorter than me, and probably close to the same age, perhaps a year older, maybe about twenty-six.

"You know you don't have to tolerate that sort of treatment?" she said.

"You don't understand." I had hoped no one had noticed. Only someone who has been in an abusive relationship can understand what it's like, and how difficult it is to get out of.

"I understand. I know what it's like. You don't deserve to be treated like that. I know you think you've no choice, but I'm going to give you one." She handed me a small piece of paper. "If you decide to leave him, I can help you."

"Caitlin's Nail Salon?" I stared at the sticker in my hand. There was also a phone number and nothing else.

"Keep that in your purse. If he sees it, he won't consider it to be threatening. Call me if you need help. I'll help you; it's what I do. You can get out of this situation safely if you want to. We operate an escape route for victims of domestic violence."

Realizing I must look like a fish, opening and closing my mouth but making no sound, I shut my mouth and said nothing; I didn't know what to say. Putting the sticker in my purse, I hurried out, glancing around to see if anyone else was staring at me with pity or disgust. Malcolm was already in a bad mood. I didn't want to give him anything more to be angry about. He still had an almost full glass of beer in front of him. I sat down and sipped my water, watching the woman from the restroom leave. I guessed her name was Caitlin.

Malcolm waved to the server, who still hadn't brought the check, gulped down his beer and stood up. As soon as the bill arrived, he grabbed it with one hand and my wrist with the other, and almost dragged me towards the cashier. As we drove home, the silence was deafening. I stared out the window, trying not to make a sound that might trigger his temper. Just before we turned the corner onto our street, I spotted Caitlin. She was going into a duplex set back a little from the road. I guess it shouldn't have surprised me, considering she'd been at the restaurant. It made sense that she lived close by. As we got out of the car and went into our apartment, I prayed Malcolm had calmed down. He hadn't.

~~

Two hours later, I was banging on what I hoped was Caitlin's back door. Although I still had her sticker with the phone number on, I no longer had my phone. Malcolm had smashed it. I hammered on the door again and heard footsteps and the key turning. As the door opened, I almost fell into the small kitchen. Caitlin caught my arm, preventing me from hitting the floor.

"Help me, please!"

Caitlin guided me to a chair and turned on the lights.

"He did this to you?"

"Yes, my boyfriend Malcolm."

"What's your name?"

"Sally."

"Hi Sally, I'm a nurse and I need to make sure you don't have any serious injuries, other than what we can see."

I hadn't looked in the mirror, but guessed from how much it hurt, and the blood all over my clothes, I must have looked bad. She examined my entire body and concluded that there were no broken bones or apparent internal damage.

"Do you want me to take you to the hospital just to be certain?"

"No! Malcolm warned me to never go near the hospital. I don't want to, and I don't need to."

"In that case, I'd like to take some photos of your injuries before I dress them. Is that alright with you?"

I nodded my head but decided that was a bad idea. It hurt too much. I wasn't sure why she wanted photos, but I also didn't care.

When she finished, she switched on the kettle and made some tea.

"I need to ask you a few questions, Sally, and I want you to be completely honest, okay?"

"Okay."

"First, why did you come to my door?"

"You gave me one of your stickers at the diner. I live just around the corner, and I saw you going into your house when we were driving past."

"Did he see you come here?"

"No, he went out, probably to the bar. He usually goes there and gets drunk after he hits me."

"Do you have any children?"

"No,"

"Do you have any family here in Austin?"

"I was born here but, the only family I have are my aunt and uncle in Cambridge, Massachusetts. I moved to live with them about ten years ago, after my parents died."

"Great, so they'll have no problem giving you a place to stay?"

"No, in fact, they'll be delighted when they hear I'm coming back. They live in a big old house close to the University—my uncle's a professor there and my aunt writes poetry." I tried not to sound too proud, though Caitlin looked impressed.

"This question's very important, Sally. Are you prepared to leave Malcolm and everything you own? If you are, I can arrange that immediately. We can take you to Cambridge. If not, your only option is to go to the police. But I'm sure you don't need me to tell you that might just make matters worse." She paused. "Will you leave him and your life now?"

I didn't hesitate. "Yes, I want nothing more to do with him. I want to go as far away as possible and never see him again. But why are you doing this for me?"

"Let me get dressed and we'll go. I'll explain on the way."

As she drove, Caitlin told me we were going to her office. Once there, she would call a person in her network, Pat. She would come and pick me up. At that point, I would be on my way to Cambridge.

Her office was a small, efficiency apartment in an enormous complex. All the buildings looked identical. She explained to me she felt it was a safer place to meet victims, as it was difficult to find anything there. It was all so impersonal.

She pulled the car into a single-car garage and closed the door as soon as she shut off the engine. We entered the apartment through a door at the back of the garage. While we waited, Caitlin told me more about the escape route and how it worked. Thirty minutes later, Pat arrived, and Caitlin waved as we drove off.

CHAPTER TWO

Thankfully, the drive from Austin to Temple was silent. The last thing I wanted to do was to take part in a trivial conversation with anyone. Pat, who was doing the driving, was also a survivor of domestic violence, so I guessed she understood how I felt. Though, if I'm being honest, I was not sure how I felt myself. It had all happened so fast.

Well, the violence and verbal abuse had been happening for some time, but the escape was unexpected and very sudden. A part of me still loved Malcolm, though I didn't understand why. Caitlin was right. I needed to get as far away from him as possible because I knew he could easily talk me into going back to him. With each beating, I hoped it would truly be the last, but there was always another one. Malcolm said it was my fault. Even if maybe it was sometimes I had to accept, I couldn't fix it. I couldn't stop making him angry. I tried. And no matter how sorry he was, nor how many times he promised never to hit me again, there would always be a next time. This last time was the worst. I thought he would never stop.

The rush hour traffic was long gone. Of course, traffic on I-35 was always busy. Enormous eighteen-wheelers sped past as Pat kept to a steady five miles below the posted speed limit. I stared out the window. There was nothing to see apart from the occasional large green sign for exits. It wasn't long before we passed the sign for Temple and Pat pulled off the interstate.

"We're here," she said as she pulled into the parking lot in front of a small, red brick apartment building.

I could still hear the trucks in the distance. Struggling to climb out of the passenger side, I stifled a groan. Every muscle ached. Pat came around and took my arm.

"Here, let me help you. After sitting still for over an hour, you'll have stiffened up. I know what it feels like," she whispered as I hobbled through the humid Texas night, towards the front door of her apartment.

I said nothing. I was too embarrassed.

Pat's apartment was small. It looked like she had furnished it with a mixture of secondhand furniture and a few items from IKEA, but it was comfortable, and above all, it was safe. She showed me to the guest room and pointed out the bathroom down the hall, then told me to sit down at the kitchen table while she made us hot chocolate.

"I've always found hot chocolate helps me to sleep. I've no idea why, because chocolate has caffeine and sugar in it. Right?" she said, placing a mug on the table in front of me, along with a small bottle of aspirin. "Take a couple of these. They'll ease the pain."

I tried to smile, but it hurt too much. I hadn't looked at my face but guessed it must look awful; it felt awful. I carefully sipped the hot drink, swallowing two of the pills.

"Take your mug to bed with you." Pat helped me to stand up. "There are clean PJs on the bed, and you can shower in the morning. Just try to get some sleep."

She led me down the hall to the bedroom. It had twin beds with a small wooden table between them, a lamp, and a box of Kleenex. I spotted a pair of pale blue cotton PJs, neatly folded on the pillow on one bed, and black sweatpants and a t-shirt on the other.

"Tomorrow we'll hit up Walmart and get some stuff for you to last until you get to your aunt and uncle's house in Cambridge."

I looked down at my once beautiful, green silk blouse, noticing the blood and dirt; my jeans also needed to be replaced. I shuddered and my legs suddenly felt like jelly. Sitting down on the end of the bed, I put my head in my hands, quickly raising it again as it hurt to touch my face.

"Thank you, Pat. I can't remember if I thanked Caitlin. Please tell her I'm truly grateful."

Pat smiled, but there were tears in her eyes. "We know—I know exactly how you feel. Good night, Sally." She closed the door quietly.

The following morning, I had difficulty getting out of bed. All my muscles appeared to have seized up. After a long, hot shower, I felt better, that is until I looked in the mirror. I'd been afraid to do that the previous night. My face was a mess. One eye was almost closed, surrounded by red and purple bruising. There was a cut under my eye that Caitlin had put some strips of sticky stuff to seal closed. Thank goodness she was a nurse, and I could avoid going to the hospital. The last thing I needed was someone calling the police. Malcolm warned me he would kill me if I ever called the police. I blinked hard to hold back the tears. No matter how hard I wished, I couldn't change him, couldn't fix him, or what had gone wrong between us. Something went wrong. I just didn't know what, so how could I fix it? We were so happy when we first met—until we weren't.

The smell of coffee distracted me and drew me to the kitchen.

"Good morning, Sally. I didn't realize your hair was so blonde. It looked almost black with all that blood in it. How're you feeling?" Pat said, studying my face. I could feel myself blushing. I couldn't believe that I'd allowed myself to get into this situation. But I was very grateful to have found a way out of it.

"A lot better after a shower, thanks."

Pat shook her head. "Try not to feel embarrassed about it, Sally. I know how easy it is to say that, and how hard it is to not feel guilty. But seriously, it's not your fault. The fault's his. He behaves that way because something is broken in him. Not in you." She poured a mug of coffee and handed it to me. "If there's anything wrong with us, it's that we fall for these men and don't leave at the first sign."

It made me feel better; she included herself; and of course, I knew she was a 'recovering victim', as Caitlin put it. She said it was like alcoholism, or any other addiction. But as with any addiction, it's possible to cure.

"As soon as I get to Cambridge, I'm going to find a good therapist," I said. Pat smiled and nodded.

"Do, it helps—okay, first things first. You need to call your family in Cambridge and let them know you're coming, and you need to call your boss and let him know you're leaving." She handed me a phone. "It's a cheap pay-as-you-go, but it's yours. Once you replace it, you can save it to give to the first victim you help along the Escape Route—the ER. If they need it. Do you know their numbers? If not, we can probably find them online."

"Thank you. Yes, fortunately numbers are my thing. I don't remember everyone, just the important ones." I took the phone and somehow the idea that I would one day do for someone else what she was doing for me made me feel a lot better.

First, I called my uncle and aunt. That was a tough conversation. It delighted them when I told them I was heading to see them. Then I explained the circumstances and my Aunt Vickie started to cry, while Uncle Bill said nothing after the first swear word I had ever heard him utter. Through her sniffling, Aunt Vickie said that he had gone out to the backyard and was pacing around like an angry lion, and they would have my bedroom ready for me. I told her I expected to be there in two days and hung up.

The call to my boss was only slightly easier. He already suspected that Malcolm and I were having problems. He'd seen bruises and had once told me I should call on him if I ever needed anything. It was no surprise, but he was very disappointed that I was leaving, though he said he understood. He also promised to mail me a check for my last month's salary plus any holiday pay due. I gave him my uncle's address.

"And Pete?"

"Yes?"

"Please don't share my address with anyone. I don't want Malcolm to get hold of it." I didn't think he would, but felt I should say it just to be certain.

"Of course, Sally. I'll keep it to myself. And please use my name for a reference."

"Thank you." I disconnected the call.

"Okay, Pat. That's done."

"I just thought of one other thing."

"What?"

"You should get on to the USPS website and set up a redirection for all your mail."

"That won't be necessary. For one thing, anything important, such as bank statements and credit card bills, is paperless. I do as much of that online as I can. And because Malcolm smashed my laptop, he can't even try to access any of it. Plus, we hadn't been together long enough to have anything joint."

After a second mug of coffee, we headed out to the store. I bought a couple of pairs of jeans, underwear, socks, and a pair of sneakers, plus some toiletries and a backpack to hold everything. Just enough to get me to Cambridge. Once I was there, I could get whatever else I needed. I was thankful that I'd thought about grabbing my purse before going to Caitlin for help. At least I had my ID and credit cards.

"What do the people who don't have any money do?" I asked Pat.

"We buy them the necessities to get them where they're going. It's part of the service. To be honest, I feel it's the very least I can do in return for the help I received. And it's Caitlin's mission in life."

We picked up some sandwiches and returned to Pat's apartment. I changed into fresh underwear, a new pair of jeans and a T-shirt. Leaving the clothes Pat had supplied in a laundry basket in the bathroom—for the next victim. Then I put my blood-stained clothes in one of the empty shopping bags and put that in the trash. Over lunch, Pat told me what to expect. She said it would be exhausting, but that I would be in Cambridge within two days.

"You said you have been through this yourself," I said. "How long did it take you to recover—to trust your own judgment again?"

Pat studied me in silence for a few minutes before answering.

"I spent several weeks at a shelter before Caitlin came along and offered me the opportunity to start living my life again. My husband, now my ex-husband, had left Texas, so I didn't need to leave. I feel incredibly lucky. But, to answer your question, I don't think I'll ever fully trust my judgment again."

"That's what I'm afraid of. I so badly want to meet someone, to start a family of my own. I think I was in too much of a hurry, and now I'm not at all sure I won't make the same mistake."

"You might. The difference is that if you do, you'll recognize it immediately and stop before it gets to a point that you're trapped—at least, that's what I'm hoping. And that's where therapy will help."

The next two days were pretty much exactly as she had described. She drove me to just north of Dallas, where we said goodbye. From there, I swapped cars and drivers so many times I can't remember. The second night on the road was a complete blur. I can't even remember where I stayed. Of course, I thanked each one of them for their help and kindness. I promised myself that I would be as kind to any victims if I were called on to do the same in the future. I was determined that I would make myself available to help in any way I could.

CHAPTER THREE

By the end of the second day, we pulled into Uncle Bill's driveway. As Pat had predicted, I was exhausted. Climbing out of the car with difficulty, I grabbed my bag from the back seat and thanked the driver once again. I seemed to remember her name was Stephanie.

"Would you like to come in? You probably need to rest before you drive back." I couldn't remember where she had actually driven from. It was all a blur, but I knew it was at least three hours away.

"No, thank you. I've friends close by. I'm going to stay overnight with them before heading home."

As she drove off, the front door opened, and Aunt Vickie ran down the steps to greet me. She hadn't changed at all. Her hair, once a deep, fiery red, but was now more gray than red. As always, she had it tied up in a complicated knot at the back of her head, with wisps escaping around her face. She had green eyes, almost the same color as mine. She was also the same height as me. People often mistook us for mother and daughter. In fact, we were not even blood relatives. She stopped a few feet away from me, staring at my face as though she didn't recognize me. Then I remembered my swollen, black eye. I hadn't told her the extent of my injuries, just that my boyfriend had become violent. She threw her arms around me and hugged me so tight I couldn't breathe.

Uncle Bill came out behind her and when he saw my face, he made a noise like a growl before also giving me a bear hug. His hair tended to stick out like Einstein's or would if he didn't keep it short. Even short, it looked like it could do with a comb. He had lost some weight, which made him look even taller. He was six foot four inches, an inch taller than my father—his brother.

Uncle Bill carried my backpack upstairs to the room that had been my bedroom since I was fifteen years old. It felt like home. I felt safe at last.

"Is this the only bag you have?" Aunt Vickie asked me, looking concerned.

"Yes, I left with nothing, Aunt Vickie. It was an Escape Route for victims of domestic violence. He beat me up, and I left the house and never went back. It would have been too dangerous, and I might not have been able to escape."

"An Escape Route?"

I nodded. "A woman approached me in a restaurant restroom when she noticed he was getting nasty. She told me she had a network of people helping victims of domestic violence. I said I was fine—I wasn't really, but I didn't believe she could help. I didn't believe anyone could help me."

"But she did?"

"Yes. On the way home, I saw her going into her house. It was just around the corner from ours—mine and my boyfriend's…"

"And?"

"That evening he was in a terrible mood. He had gotten into trouble at work and when he gets angry, he takes it out on me—he used to. He started getting rough. No matter what I did or said, he just got angrier. Then he punched me and when I curled up on the floor—I usually did that when he hit me and it stopped him—that time he didn't stop, he kicked me."

"He kicked you!" Aunt Vickie gasped, sitting down on the bed with her hand over her heart. "He *kicked* you?" She repeated.

"Usually? You mean he did this before?" Uncle Bill said.

I nodded. "After he left, I ran around the corner to Caitlin's house—that's her name—she told me not to go home, to just leave right then and there, so I did."

"I'm glad you did. We can replace your things. We can never replace you." Aunt Vickie wiped a tear as it rolled down her cheek.

"Do you think he'll follow you here?" Uncle Bill asked.

"He doesn't know about you. He showed no interest in my life before I met him. I learned early on not to ask him about his family. When I did, he went into a black mood."

"That's so strange, but lucky," Aunt Vickie said. "We'll go shopping in the morning. Get some sleep now." She hugged me.

~~

When I woke up, for a second I didn't remember where I was. Looking around the familiar room, it all came back to me. I was home. My aunt had kept my bedroom exactly as it was when I lived there. It was a teenager's room. This big, old, beautiful house had been home to me since my parents died. It was very close to the university where Uncle Bill worked and where I got my degree. My bedroom was at the top of the house with a small turret in one corner where my desk was. It was always so easy to study there, surrounded by windows. My uncle's office was on the same floor, and there was a bathroom and a spare bedroom. The next floor down, the second floor, was the main suite. It comprised an enormous bedroom with a quiet sitting area to one side and an ensuite bathroom. Aunt Vickie's office was the only other room on that floor. It overlooked their enormous back yard. She said the flowers and trees gave her inspiration as she wrote. She was an accomplished poet.

After a long, hot shower, I joined Aunt Vickie in the kitchen, poured myself a cup of coffee, and perched on a stool at the breakfast bar.

"How're you feeling this morning?" Aunt Vickie said, studying my injured eye. "It looks less swollen, but even more colorful today. I still can't see your beautiful green eyes; they're so bloodshot."

"It looks worse than it feels. At least it no longer hurts to smile, so that's good."

"Still finding silver linings, I see," Uncle Bill said, coming in and sitting beside me. "Good to see you're feeling better."

"As soon as we've had breakfast, we're heading to the mall, Bill. We should be back before lunch," Aunt Vickie said, putting a plate of bacon and eggs in front of each of us.

"Take your time, dear. I've work to do, and I can take care of myself."

Three hours later, I was back in my bedroom pulling things out of bags, removing tags and putting away my new clothes. When Aunt Vickie walked into the room, I jumped and let out a yelp. My heart was beating so fast I had to sit down and take a deep breath.

"Are you alright, dear?" Aunt Vickie eyed me with concern.

"Yes, I just got a fright, sorry." I stood up and gathered up the empty bags, stuffed tissue paper and tags into one and folded the others, stuffing them all into the same bag.

"Let me take all that trash. I'll put it in the recycle." As she studied my face, Aunt Vickie said, "Are you sure you're alright?"

"I'm just a little on edge. I'll get over it." Despite my effort to smile, I remained uncomfortable. I wondered if I would ever get over that feeling of danger when someone walked into the room. *Would I always expect the worst?*

"Sally, your aunt and I have been talking and we think it might be a good idea if you considered therapy?" Uncle Bill said as we cleared the table after dinner that evening.

"Actually, Caitlin recommended that too," I said. "I plan to look into it."

"Oh good. I wasn't sure how you would feel about it. I spoke to my friend Matt. He's the professor of psychology, and he's given me a couple of names."

"Thanks Uncle Bill. I appreciate that. That's something I'll follow up on and make an appointment. I do want to get back to work, but I don't feel quite ready to face interviewing right now, so therapy would definitely help."

"You probably won't really appreciate how much trauma you're dealing with until you start therapy." Uncle Bill pulled an index card out of his pocket and handed it to me. "Matt said to try the first one and see if he'll work for you. He said it's always useful to have a second choice in case the first is not compatible—the second one is female in case you're less comfortable with a man."

"Yeah, I'll probably try her first. I'm not sure what to expect—but everyone seems to think it's essential."

"Oh, I'm sure the therapist will explain the process to you on your first visit. And yes, healing the mind is every bit as important as healing the body. In fact, probably more important. Don't you agree, Bill?" Aunt Vickie looked at Uncle Bill, who nodded vigorously.

I wasn't looking forward to it, but I was determined to do whatever it took to get my life back on track. So many people had done so much to help me, it was time I started trying to help myself.

CHAPTER FOUR

My first therapy session was a disaster. I made an appointment with Olga, the female therapist. Somehow, I believed a woman would be less intimidating—more empathetic. I expected she would be capable of understanding how I allowed myself to be a victim.

At nine o'clock in the morning, I was in the waiting room in a small house set back from the road. The only thing that differentiated it from a dental appointment was the lack of that chemical scent and the absence of the background sound of the drill. That and the fact that the waiting room was like a shabby sitting room, in some neglected bed-and-breakfast. The fear was every bit as strong as the fear of having a tooth pulled.

A woman with brown hair, going gray, pulled back into a tight bun at the back of her neck, stuck her head around the door of the waiting room. No crisp white coat. A long gray skirt and raspberry colored cotton blouse, buttoned up to the neck.

"Miss Simms?" I was the only person in the room. I followed her across the hall, and she closed the door behind us.

There, in front of me, was the inevitable couch. It was as scary a sight as that hydraulic chair with the angled lamp and the drill dangling above it. My stomach was a tight knot and the only reason I could sit on the couch was because my knees gave way, and I couldn't remain standing. But lie down I could not do. I could not make myself so vulnerable, so exposed, and yes, look foolish. Olga sat in a winged armchair on one side of the couch, saying nothing.

I sat there waiting for some sign of what she expected of me. After all, I had no previous experience. I only knew what I had seen in the movies, and that might not be the reality. I fully expected some sort of instruction from the therapist, as Aunt Vickie had suggested. Hoping for a soft, sympathetic voice to say something like "please lie down on the couch and tell me all about your childhood—" or anything that would help to get me started. To be perfectly honest, I really didn't know why I was there, other than everyone said it would help. I knew I needed help, but I didn't know why I needed it. I assumed that was what the therapist would tell me.

My mother had instilled in me a firm belief that both whining and boasting were equally abhorrent. Being an analytical and introverted child, and because I wanted to please her, I probably took these lessons to extremes. This was something I had to come to terms with before therapy could begin. How could I open up to a complete stranger about my life without either whining or boasting, or both?

The silence continued, and of course, the longer it lasted, the harder it became to break. The therapist's half smile, which, in my very stressed state, I interpreted as a sneer, didn't help. I think I probably sat there for 15 minutes. It felt much longer than that. Finally, in desperation, I jumped to my feet and ran out the door.

It was two weeks before I regained enough courage to try again. This time, I called the male therapist Rick Brown, the one my uncle's friend had recommended. I made another appointment, with a better idea of what to expect—nothing, no words of encouragement, no help at all. I was going to have to do this on my own.

I was uncomfortable with the fact that both therapists were part of the same practice. At least they shared the same waiting room, so I assumed they were. Once again, I was the only person there. Rick came in and asked me to follow him into the next room.

Though I didn't want to, I lay down on the couch; I did not relax. I was so tense my body almost hovered above the couch. But I didn't pause, not to draw breath, not even to think. I started talking. On my way to his rooms, I'd practiced what I was going to say. I started by telling him of my previous traumatic attempt at therapy. To my relief, he didn't smile, and he responded with a sympathetic look and nodded his head. However, that was all I could think of to say.

"So, what made you decide on therapy?"

"My uncle recommended it."

"Why?"

"Because I've just escaped from an abusive relationship. I guess he believes I need to figure out why I allowed that to happen. I suppose he feels you can help me do that?"

"Well, I think the fact that you escaped is a good sign. Start at the beginning and we'll work together to figure out why it happened, and what the lesson is. Everything that happens to us, good or bad, has a lesson. Our job is to identify that lesson and learn it."

We agreed on twice weekly sessions. And, for the next six months, every Tuesday and Thursday, I lay down on that couch and talked. About how I met Malcolm; about my promotion at the bank and how it angered him, because I didn't deserve it.

"Why do you say that?" He interrupted.

"Well, because Malcolm told me."

"And did they demote you when you couldn't perform?"

"No. I—" I thought about that for a moment. "I guess I did okay. Pete, my boss, promised to give me a good reference."

"Okay, continue."

Before I left on that day, Rick suggested I look into any courses related to my work.

"It'll be good for you to keep up with the market, and to exercise your brain. It'll also distract you from dwelling on the past."

~~

That evening, I mentioned what Rick had said.

"Great idea!" Uncle Bill said. "It'll help to keep your resume looking good. Fill in the gap created by this relocation."

After dinner, I sat with him, in front of his computer in his study, and we searched for a suitable course.

"With your existing degrees, you could probably complete many of these Financial Consultant Certifications in less than six months."

"I would like to do one online, but Rick was firm about it being in person. Something to do with 'getting back in the water', he said."

"That makes sense to me. Let me talk to my colleagues. I'm sure we can find something."

Over dinner the following evening, Uncle Bill told me he had a couple of recommendations.

"The one that I think is the absolute best is starting next week. It's in the University and sounds ideal. In fact, Owen—he's one of the professors in the business school—was so enthusiastic about it, I put your name down. I hope you don't mind. He said it was filling up fast." His face creased with concern. "I know you can do this yourself, and you can cancel it if you're not interested. I wanted to be sure you had the option."

"Of course, I don't mind. Thank you. I know you were not trying to take over." I looked at the leaflet he handed me. "It looks perfect. Definitely, I'll follow up on this one." I hugged him.

For the next few months, my days were full. Two mornings a week of therapy, two full days of lectures and the rest of the week, I was in the library studying. A bonus was the fact that everything was within walking distance. Uncle Bill bought the house because it was close to the University. He preferred to walk when he could, rather than drive. I had developed the same habit when I came to live with them. It felt very healing to be back in the University where I had been so happy before.

I hoped I could make friends during the course as well. Perhaps even meet a man. Although I was nervous about dating again, I wanted to find that special someone. Someone to share my life with. I wanted a family of my own. I wanted an opportunity to prove to myself that I could get it right.

I made some friends. We formed a study group, met in the library, and kept each other on track. Three girls and myself. No men. In fact, it was a small class and there were only two guys in the entire class, and they were both married.

Rick was right, of course. The course was challenging, and it kept me distracted from feeling sorry for myself. My instincts were to stay home and hide. I still felt so embarrassed about the stupid decisions I had made. How long it took me to make that one sensible decision and get out. I probably wouldn't have done it without Caitlin's intervention. But having human interaction was clearly exactly what I needed. I somehow expected people to look at me and know how stupid I was, even with the bruises gone. It was as though I had a sign on my head. I discovered it was inside my head and no one else was aware, except Rick, who didn't judge me and was helping me to understand and heal.

Therapy was definitely more challenging than the course. Sometimes a simple question from Rick would open up memories I didn't even know were there.

"Why do you think your parents' marriage was so happy?"

"Because sometimes I felt like I was in the way, that they were so happy with each other, they just didn't need me around. And I once asked my mother how they had such a good relationship, when so many of my friend's parents were divorced. She told me it was hard work. You had to work at it every day and be prepared to compromise."

"Do you think you're trying to recreate your parents' relationship?"

All that day, I thought about it. I could remember my parents sometimes arguing, but never for very long. They always listened to each other's point of view, and yes, compromised. I didn't understand Rick's question. Yes, I wanted to have a relationship as good as theirs, but I didn't think I was trying to recreate theirs—but perhaps I was.

CHAPTER FIVE

As winter turned to spring, I graduated from both therapy and the financial consultant course. Rick made me promise to return if I ever felt the need to talk, or if I had any concerns at all. I agreed I would, although I felt ready to get back to real life.

The day after my graduation, I sat down at the desk in my bedroom and started making a list of what I needed to do.

The first item on my list was to get a laptop. A knock on my bedroom door interrupted my thoughts.

"Come in."

Uncle Bill stuck his head around the door. "Now that you're feeling the benefit of therapy and are ready to start your job search, I have this old laptop that might be of use to you," he said. "I realize I probably should have given you this before you started the course. I just didn't think about it."

"You must have been reading my thoughts!" I took the laptop from him and gave him a hug. "Luckily, my resume is almost up to date and stored online, in the cloud, so with this I can start my job search immediately. The library was okay for studying, but I definitely need a computer at home. Thank you!"

"It's a bit old, so slow, but it still works."

"That's all I need for now. And I managed the course without it." I started setting it up as Uncle Bill headed back to his study.

~~

By the end of the afternoon, I'd written a cover letter, polished my resume and added my most recent boss, Pete, as a reference, along with the end date for my last position. I also added the financial consultant certification I'd just received; the start and end dates for that course neatly filled in the gap since I left Austin.

I had compiled a list of five banks to apply to, and sent off my resume and cover letter to my top three choices. Although I had been assistant manager at my last job, the positions I applied for were all for tellers. I wanted to ease back into working again. I knew I could do a teller's job.

"How is the job search going?" Uncle Bill asked as we sat down for dinner.

"Not bad. Thanks again for the laptop. I've applied to three banks in the area and have a list of alternatives if nothing comes of them."

"It's good that there are three assistant manager positions available." Aunt Vickie said as she helped herself to some mashed potatoes.

"No, I applied for teller jobs."

"Teller? Why on earth would you do that?" Uncle Bill said. "With your qualifications and experience you should be manager, but at least assistant manager."

"Well, I don't have that much experience. They only promoted me to assistant manager three months before I left, and Malcolm said—"

"Malcolm said!" Uncle Bill almost shouted, continuing in a quieter tone after a sharp look from Aunt Vickie. "Malcolm said? Given the way he behaved, I'm surprised you even listened to him. He was most likely jealous that you got the promotion instead of him—if you ask me—"

"Once you get a job, I'm sure they'll see your value and promote you," Aunt Vickie said. "Anyone want gravy?" She continued holding up the gravy boat expectantly.

I shook my head, amused by her effort to change the subject. Uncle Bill was easily excited, but he was well meaning. He'd always been one of my favorite people since long before I ever came to live with them. He and my dad were very close and as he and Aunt Vickie never had children, they lavished attention on me.

"Hopefully, I'll at least get a couple of interviews. By the way, if I do, is it okay for me to borrow one of your cars?"

"You can use mine anytime you wish, my dear," Aunt Vickie said.

"A car! Of course, we'll need to get you a car. You can use one of ours, of course, but you'll need your own, eventually. Let's do that tomorrow," Uncle Bill said. "Splendid dinner, as usual, Vickie. Thanks." He stood up, and I helped him to clear the table while Aunt Vickie stacked the dishwasher.

~~

Next morning Uncle Bill insisted on taking me to his dealership and two hours later I drove home in a lightly used Ford hybrid. He wanted to get a new car, but I put my foot down. I insisted I would pay him back and didn't want to incur that big a debt. He finally gave in.

I hadn't needed a car in Texas. Well, I—we had one that we shared. We both paid for it, but Malcolm drove it. As we both worked at the same bank, we really didn't need two cars. I didn't know what became of it but was not about to attempt to find out; I certainly couldn't take it when it was shared property, and the loan was in Malcolm's name, so leaving it cost me nothing.

When I got home, I did some more job searching. Uncle Bill was right. That laptop was slow. When it finally booted up, I started a list of all the things I would need to get as I rebuilt my life. It was a long list; I fiddled around with it, trying to order it by priority, but finally gave up and returned to my first task: finding work. I pulled up the possibilities I'd identified and opened my email. As I watched the stream of incoming email, it surprised me to see a response to one of my applications from the previous day. Even more surprising was the fact that it was a request to complete the enclosed form and set up an appointment for an interview.

I finished reading through my email and deleted most of it. An hour later, I joined Aunt Vickie in the kitchen to help her with dinner.

"You look pleased with yourself," she said, smiling. "Happy with your car?"

"I'm delighted with the car, but even better is that I've got an interview scheduled for tomorrow with my first choice."

"That's great news!" Aunt Vickie hugged me.

"It's quite close to here, so close to everything, really." I hoped it wasn't too obvious how nervous I was. I'd already caused them so much stress, I didn't want to add to that.

Getting back into real life was a daunting idea. I knew I had to do it, but it would not be easy.

~~

I was up early the following day. My interview was not until ten, but I was too excited to stay in bed. Instead, I read over the application form I'd submitted and even looked through my resume, though if there was a mistake in that, it was way too late now.

I dressed in one of the business outfits I'd bought and a pair of comfortable shoes with small heels that Aunt Vickie had given me. Luckily, we wore the same size because I didn't want to wear new shoes for an interview. The situation was already making me uncomfortable. I hated interviewing, no matter which side of the desk I was sitting on. At least I could ensure my feet were not sore. I spent some time applying make-up and doing my hair. It had grown even longer over the last six months, and the blonde highlights created by the constant Texas sun had dulled. It was all now just a dirty blonde. I made a mental note to make an appointment to get it cut to a more manageable length; and another mental note to add that to my list of things to do.

The bank was in an old redbrick building, with enormous granite columns on either side of the imposing timber doors embedded with iron studs and hinges. Arriving at nine forty-five, I parked in an underground parking lot across the street. Although the bank was within walking distance, I had driven, to avoid arriving hot and sweaty, or in any way disheveled. A tall, thin woman with gray hair and a gentle smile showed me into a small office off the main foyer.

"Mark will be with you in a few minutes. Can I get you some water or coffee?"

"No, I'm fine thanks." I sat down and reminded myself to breathe—slowly and deeply.

A few minutes later, the door opened again, and a tall, well-built man came in.

"Hi, Sally? I'm Mark Brennan, the Manager here." We shook hands, and he sat down on the other side of the desk.

CHAPTER SIX

Two hours later, as I drove home, the interview replayed in my head. Mark was very good looking, with dark brown eyes, blond hair and a well-trimmed beard, actually more like he hadn't shaved for two days, but had kept the growth tidy. Almost too good looking. Malcolm was very good looking. He was taller than Malcolm, who, at five foot ten, was only a couple of inches taller than me. Mark was at least six foot two. I'm not sure why I felt the need to compare them. I guess I'd gotten into the habit of comparing every man I met to Malcolm. Hopefully, that was a good sign—if it helped me to avoid ever getting involved with another abusive man.

It surprised me when he told me he'd already talked to my last boss, Pete. He said Pete gave me a glowing reference, but he wanted to know why I was applying for a teller position if I had been an assistant manager before. I explained to him I needed a job immediately and knew that it would be easier to find a teller position. Hopefully, that convinced him. I didn't want to tell him I was afraid I was not good enough to do the job of assistant manager. Anyway, he said he would get back to me, so I guessed I needed to keep looking.

Aunt Vickie and Uncle Bill were in the kitchen having lunch when I got home.

"How did it go?" They both said, in unison, followed by some ritual they went through every time they did that; it happened a lot. They hooked their little fingers on their right hands together and closed their eyes. I guess if you have been married as long as they have, spent all your time together, and enjoyed each other's company, you would develop silly rituals. I knew from experience they were making a wish and waited for them to open their eyes before answering, helping myself to some of the salad from a bowl on the counter.

"It seemed to go well. He asked me why I was looking for a position as a teller when I had been an AM. Hopefully, I answered that question to his satisfaction."

"I think I asked you this before, but why are you not looking for an assistant manager position?" Uncle Bill said, his eyebrows drawn together and his head to one side as he looked at me.

"Yes, you asked me that before. I told you, because I just don't have the self-confidence right now. Perhaps once I get back in the swing of work. Like I said, Malcolm told me I wasn't good enough. That they would fire me, or demote me, as soon as they figured out I didn't know what I was doing."

"That's the same Malcolm who did that to your face?" Aunt Vickie said, pointing to my eye, which had long since healed at that stage, though I still had a small scar. "I don't think he had your best interests in mind."

"Well, they already have an AM. It's much easier to get a job as a teller," I said. "Anyway, I'm going to go send out a few more applications just in case I don't get this one."

I put my plate and fork in the dishwasher and headed up to my room, hoping they would not keep on at me about not looking for an AM position.

~~

I was having coffee with Aunt Vickie the following morning when my phone rang.

"It's them—the bank," I said as I answered it. Aunt Vickie stopped what she was doing and turned to watch me.

"Hello—Hi Mark, yes, I'm free to talk." I looked at Aunt Vickie and took a deep breath. She didn't move. "Yes, certainly—yes—okay, yes, that's a good email address. Okay, thanks." I hung up.

"Well?" Aunt Vickie almost yelled.

"He's sending me a job offer. If I agree with the terms, I'm to sign it and return it." I jumped off the stool and threw my arms around her as we jumped up and down.

"What a relief! I must go upstairs and check my email." I almost ran up to my room. By the time I sat at my desk and logged in, the offer was waiting for me. I read through it quickly. It looked good. Then I settled down to read it more carefully.

The important details like salary and benefits looked pretty standard and acceptable. I'd already mentioned that I would need a few weeks to find an apartment and get moved in, so the suggested start date was a full month away, which was perfect. I unplugged the laptop and carried it across the hall to Uncle Bill's office. He opened the door before I had a chance to knock. Aunt Vickie was in there with him. Obviously, she'd told him, and they were waiting for me. I passed him the laptop.

"The offer looks good to me, standard stuff, with a start date a month away."

He sat down and read through it slowly, nodding his head. "Yes, I agree, all standard stuff. What do you think?"

"I'm going to take it. I know you think I should look for an AM position, but really, I feel more comfortable with this right now. Maybe, like I said, after I regain my confidence, I might find the strength to consider it, just not now." I hoped he would just let it go.

I watched as he took a breath and opened his mouth, but he closed it quickly when he caught Aunt Vickie's stern look. I managed to avoid smiling. *How lucky I am to have such wonderful people in my life.*

~~

I signed the offer letter and sent it back to Mark. I felt I had to do it immediately before I chickened out. So much had changed in six months, and even more in just this last week. I couldn't believe it. It still felt strange to be back in Cambridge, about to start a new job and to look for a new home, all with no planning or consideration. It was like someone waved a magic wand and, hey presto, I was transported into a completely new life without even a to-do list.

There was a tap on my door, and Aunt Vickie stuck her head in. "You doing okay?" she said.

"Better than okay. I can't believe how lucky I am."

"Lucky? Only you would consider it lucky to be beaten to a pulp by your boyfriend. A man who claimed to love you and then forced to run for your life." She sat down on the end of my bed, shaking her head.

"For a start, I was lucky he didn't kill me. I thought he was going to at one point. It was lucky that Caitlin was there and offered to help me. Seeing her go into her house when I did was also very lucky. I knew where she lived just when I needed help. Otherwise, I would not have been able to contact her. Malcolm had smashed my phone. I was so very lucky to have you and Uncle Bill to run to. Pat—the girl who drove me from Austin to Temple, and then to Dallas. She spent weeks in a shelter for battered women before Caitlin reached out to help her. So many women don't have the support that I do." I paused. Aunt Vickie nodded, but said nothing. "And I'm lucky that I have a degree and marketable skills."

"Okay. I guess if you look at it that way, you're lucky. I still think it would have been much luckier to have never met that man in the first place."

"Rick said that sometimes what happens to us happens because we have a lesson to learn. I just need to figure out what the lesson is—and learn it."

"Very philosophical. You always were a bit of a Pollyanna. It's one of the many things I love about you." Aunt Vickie smiled and stood up. "I guess the next thing's finding you an apartment. Though you know you're welcome to stay here as long as you like."

"I know, and I appreciate it, but I need to get my own place and get back to some sort of normal. I started making a list of what I need to do. Once I've completed and prioritized that, we can go over it."

"Okay dear, let's do that this evening over dinner."

~~

I looked at my list one last time before I headed down to dinner. Of course, I edited it slightly. I knew that my uncle and aunt would seriously question item number seven '*sign up for an online dating app*'. There is no way they would understand that. I didn't want to get into a conversation with them about it.

My list for discussion with them was:
1. *Find an apartment*
2. *Furnish apartment (minimum required)*
3. *Move in*

4. Grocery shopping
5. Buy more clothes for work
6. Update contact information with Caitlin & Pat

It's not that I thought I would forget to do any of these things. I've always felt more comfortable having a list.

"Why do you need to tell Caitlin and Pat your address?" Aunt Vickie asked.

"Because I'm now part of their network, I agreed to do whatever I can. If any victim needs to pass through this area, they may ask me to help."

Uncle Bill looked up from his copy of the list. "I love that idea. I'm sure helping other victims will be very healing for you. Let us know if you ever need any help from us."

I blinked away the tears I could feel forming in my eyes.

"Thank you. Like I said to Aunt Vickie earlier, I'm so very lucky."

"We'll get started on the apartment search first thing in the morning." Aunt Vickie said as she cleared the table.

I stood up to help her when my phone pinged. A message from Pat!

Pat: Hi Sally, are you free to talk?

I immediately called her. "Hi Pat, what's up?"

"Is there any chance you could help? We've a victim on the way to Bangor, Maine. She'll be in New York tomorrow and I was wondering if you could pick her up there and drive her to Bangor? I think the distances are manageable from where you are?"

"Absolutely no problem at all, Pat. I can pick her up tomorrow, she can stay overnight here—" I glanced at Uncle Bill, who was listening. He nodded vigorously. "—and I'll drive her up to Bangor the following day."

"Oh, that would be great. Thank you so much. I wasn't sure if you would be available, and I didn't know if you even had transport."

"No need to thank me, not after all you have done for me. I'm delighted to help. And yes, I've a car and my uncle and aunt are happy to help too."

I wrote the address and phone number Pat gave me on the top of my list before hanging up.

"You were just talking about that a minute ago," Aunt Vickie said.

"That's how I knew you wouldn't mind if I offered for her to stay here overnight," I replied. "We can put off the apartment hunting until

I get back."

"I'll make a list of possibilities while you're gone and set up appointments. That'll save time and keep me busy," Aunt Vickie said.

"I'm going to head to bed. I'll leave first thing in the morning. It should take about four hours to get there, I think?"

"Yes, that's about right. Be sure and take a break before heading back," Uncle Bill said as I headed off to bed.

"I will," I called back.

As I lay in bed, I thought about my journey from Austin to Cambridge. I went over the bits that I could remember. It felt so good to know that tomorrow I could help someone in the same situation, to make it out of the misery and pain and into a new life. Or, perhaps, like me, return to her old life and try to repair some of the damage.

CHAPTER SEVEN

I was up early the next morning and on the road. Aunt Vickie had packed some snacks and a thermos of coffee, so unless I needed a bathroom break, there would be no reason to stop. I had checked the address and planned my route before going to bed, and the tank was full.

The drive to New York was uneventful and my GPS guided me flawlessly to the correct address. I was to meet up with Grace and a guy called Ted, who was driving her from Philly. I pulled into the driveway of a small house surrounded by trees on the outskirts of White Plains. As I approached the front door, it opened, and an elderly woman called to me.

"Come in dear, Ted and Grace are here and we're about to have lunch. Please join us." She held the door open for me. "I'm Joanna, I'm a friend of Ted's aunt and you're Sally? We're in here," she said as she led me into the kitchen.

"Thank you for making the drive, Sally," Ted said, getting up, and we shook hands.

Grace just nodded to me, and half smiled. She had a bruise on the side of her chin and her left arm was in a sling. I sighed and tried to look like I wasn't shaking with a mixture of anger and fear. Not that long ago, I was in exactly the same position as this poor girl, and I knew exactly how she felt. Hell, the small scar under my eye would always remind me.

As Joanna put out a bowl of thick vegetable soup and a large glass of iced water, I sat down.

"I'm sure you could do with a bit of a rest before you head back to Boston—that's where you came from, right?"

"Cambridge, just outside Boston, yes. And yes. I would appreciate the opportunity to rest a bit before heading back, though it was a very easy drive," I said, nodding. Looking at Grace, I said. "We'll stay in Cambridge tonight and head to Bangor in the morning, if that's okay with you, Grace?"

"Thank you, Sally. Yes, that's fine with me."

~~

A little over an hour later, Ted left to return to Philly, and Grace and I said goodbye to Joanna and headed back to Cambridge.

"Just make yourself comfortable, Grace. If you want to doze off, that's fine with me. If you want to talk, I'm also cool with that. Just know I've been in that seat myself, and not very long ago. Okay?" I said as I started the engine and waved to Joanna, who was standing on her doorstep waving.

"Thank you, Sally," Grace said, also waving. "I would really like to talk, if you don't mind. I've a few questions and I wasn't comfortable asking Ted."

"Absolutely."

"How long ago did you escape?"

I thought for a moment. "Six months. Hard to believe it was that long."

"And do you miss your boyfriend—husband?"

"My boyfriend, we weren't married, thank goodness. And yes, sometimes I miss him. Despite all the cuts and bruises and six months of therapy. It's the good times that I miss. The 'what could have been' if that makes sense? I guess I miss being in love."

Grace was quiet for a few minutes. "Yeah. That's what I'm afraid of. I just can't go through any more of the pain. And I really don't know how much damage he's done to me emotionally. I mean, will I ever be able to have a proper relationship? How do you know that the next guy won't be just as bad? If you didn't recognize it the first time?"

"The only thing I can tell you, Grace, is as soon as you get settled, find a good therapist, and go; spill everything out. It works. Yes, it's painful. It's like having teeth pulled, but it works. What I discovered is that it wasn't my fault. It wasn't necessarily Malcolm's fault, although he was violent, and that was his fault. But things that happened to us in our past—our childhood—caused us to accept certain behaviors and to react as we did; sometimes things that we misinterpreted. We have to reach way back to understand and untangle the past before we can fix the present and hope for the future. I believe my big mistake was trying to convince myself that Malcolm could be what I wanted him to be. Not seeing him for who he really was. I didn't believe that any man would be so abusive—I thought all men were perfect, like my father." I don't know where that came from, but it suddenly made me feel better and I hoped Grace did, too. "I think I'm ready to get back into a relationship and trust that I'll allow no one to treat me that way again. Never make the excuses I used to make. Never again forgive the unforgivable."

"I don't know if doing that's being brave or foolish," Grace muttered.

I wasn't sure about that either. Wasn't even sure I believed what I had just said. I hoped it was true. I wanted to believe it, but more than that, I wanted to make Grace feel better if I could.

We drove most of the rest of the way back to Cambridge in silence, each of us lost in our own thoughts. Aunt Vickie had the guest room ready for Grace and dinner was cooking when we got there.

Next morning, as we got ready to head to Bangor, Aunt Vickie handed me a packed lunch and a thermos of coffee, just as she had done the day before. Grace thanked her for everything, and Aunt Vickie hugged her and told her to take care of herself, and we set off for Maine.

Grace let out a sigh. I smiled at her and said, "Don't worry, you'll eventually pay it all back by helping other victims. I promise you. It makes us feel better. We can finally do that ourselves—you're helping me to feel better about all the help I received." She nodded but said nothing. I knew how she felt.

The drive was much easier than the previous day. The closer we got to Bangor, the less tense Grace appeared to be. At one point, she opened the passenger window and took a deep, slow breath. She saw me glancing at her and smiled.

"There's nothing quite like the smell of home," she whispered and started to close the window again.

"You can leave it open if you want to," I said. "The road's quiet, and I agree, it smells good."

There was a smell of cut grass mingled with trees and something I couldn't put my finger on. It was a mixture of the smells of wild forest, small farms, and the ocean.

"I've never been to Maine before," I said.

"Really? That's surprising, considering you live so close."

"I grew up in Texas. In Austin. I only moved to Cambridge when I was fifteen. My parents died in a car crash. After that, it was all studying to get through school and get my degree. As soon as I graduated, I moved back to Austin."

"Is that where you met your boyfriend—if you don't mind me asking?" Grace said.

"I don't mind. And yes. When I graduated from Harvard, I needed to get away from Cambridge." I paused for a moment, thinking about that decision and the disastrous results. "I'd just broken up with a guy I'd been dating all through college. I went back to Texas—because my father was born there, and I thought I could meet someone like him. I got a job in a bank—my major was finance. Malcolm worked in the same bank. I guess I should have stayed in Cambridge. Not only was he violent, he constantly told me I was no good at my job. He totally undermined my confidence—I guess he was jealous of the fact that I had a degree. He went straight into the bank from high school."

"I know what you mean. I wish I had stayed in Bangor."

"Well, my therapist said that no experience is wasted if we can learn and grow from it."

"Did you really feel that therapy helped you?"

"Absolutely. I strongly recommend you start therapy before you do anything else. And if you don't like the first therapist, keep changing till you find one that works for you."

Grace nodded as she took another deep, slow breath before closing the window.

Grace's parents lived in a small town a few miles east of Bangor. As we pulled into the driveway, her parents and two young boys, her brothers, she said, came bursting out the front door and all stood by the passenger door. The two boys were literally jumping up and down like puppies. Her father stood back as her mother rushed forward and threw her arms around her, tears pouring down her cheeks. When she eventually let go, her father stepped forward and hugged her, then held her at arm's length and studied her face for a full minute, before speaking.

"Is your wrist broken?" he asked, pointing to the sling.

Grace nodded, saying nothing, while her mother sniffed loudly and dabbed her eyes with a tissue.

"Stop crying, sweetie. She's home safe now." He turned to me. "You must be Sally. Thank you so much for transporting her all that way. Please come on in." He led the way into the house.

After lunch and a walk around the town with Grace and her father, I was once again on the road heading back to Cambridge. Grace's father spent some time questioning both of us about our experiences and the Escape Route. He told Grace that he would put her in touch with a therapist friend the following day.

"Sally's right. Therapy is essential if you're not only going to minimize the trauma but also maximize the lesson," he said to her.

When I arrived home, I felt both exhausted and happy. Before leaving Bangor, I called Pat to let her know Grace was safely home. She thanked me. I told her I would be happy to help anytime.

CHAPTER EIGHT

Over breakfast the next morning, I told Aunt Vickie and Uncle Bill about my trip up to Bangor and my conversation with Grace.

"I can't believe that so much of this is going on. We just never hear about it," Aunt Vickie said.

"Most people are too afraid, or too ashamed, to admit it's happening to them. Quite a few, me included, try to convince themselves that it'll stop, and everything will go back to the way it was."

Aunt Vickie shook her head slowly. I could see she still didn't really understand.

"I guess Bill and I are lucky that neither of us were like that—Okay, let's look at apartments for you."

She produced a list of five apartments in the area. As promised, she'd been busy while I was gone. We looked through them; marking each one with a score out of ten.

"This one's definitely top of my list." I said, pointing to the cheapest on the list. They were all expensive, but anything near the University was going to be pricey.

"I actually like that one too, even if it's the cheapest." Aunt Vickie said. "The house has character, and it's on a pleasant street."

"Yes, and I could actually walk to work. Let's go see it."

~~

Two hours later, the agent opened the door to what was once a single-family mansion on a tree-lined street.

"The owner renovated the entire house. He divided it into apartments. You're the first to view it, so you get your pick." He held the door open for us. "This main entrance gives access to six apartments, and the basement is the seventh, with its own entrance. Finally, on the side of the house is the eighth unit. That one has a separate entrance, too. I'll show you that last—keep the best for last." He chuckled as though he had made a joke. I caught Aunt Vickie rolling her eyes and nudged her with my elbow as we waited for him to show us into the first unit. Finally, he led us around to the side of the house and opened the door to the separate apartment.

As I stepped through the door, it felt as though I'd come home. There was still a faint smell of fresh paint, plain white walls and light-colored wood floors. No furniture and no actual personality, but it felt right. I loved that it had its own entrance.

"This'll work," I said.

"Let's just look around. Which way's the kitchen?" Aunt Vickie asked.

"This way, ladies."

The kitchen had a stove, one less thing to purchase, and the cabinets went all the way to the ceiling, which was quite high. Lots of storage. There was a door from the kitchen out into a tiny private patio area surrounded by high walls separating it from the main backyard.

"What do you think?" He looked directly at me.

"Yes. Definitely. I want it."

~~

Over dinner, I described the apartment to Uncle Bill.

"It's in a really old, renovated house, but it has its own entrance, away from the other apartments. It's like it was built onto the side of the house as an afterthought. There's a sitting room, kitchen and half bath downstairs, and a bedroom and bathroom upstairs. This's the first let since the renovation, so it has no personality. I can make it whatever I want."

"What about furniture and other stuff?"

"Aunt Vickie's going to give me some of her old sheets and towels, and we went to IKEA and bought a few things. Just the minimum. A bed, a dining table and four chairs, a couch and a TV stand. That sort of thing. There's a stove in the kitchen, but I still need to get a refrigerator and a dishwasher, and, of course, a TV."

"We're going to get the appliances tomorrow," Aunt Vickie said.

"And when do you move in?"

"Next week!" I told him. "I'm so excited!"

"What? To be leaving us?" He smiled.

"You know that isn't what I meant."

"I know. It's time for you to get on with your life. I'm happy you found a place you like." He patted my shoulder, and, not for the first time, I thought how lucky I was to have them in my life.

~~

A week later, while waiting for the furniture to be delivered, I was sitting on the floor of my new apartment, making a list of all the things I hadn't realized I would need. Earlier, the delivery team had brought the refrigerator and dishwasher and installed them. I knew that as soon as my furniture arrived, I was going to have to assemble everything. Hence the list. I'd borrowed Uncle Bill's toolbox in order to put the furniture together, but I would need to get my own. Of course, he offered to come over and help me, but I wanted to do this myself. And I knew from experience that he wasn't great with his hands. I would be quicker on my own.

I thought about all the things I'd left behind when I walked out on Malcolm. Well, to be correct, I staggered out, bruised and bleeding. The memory made me shiver. I'd set up a similar apartment on my own before I started dating Malcolm. When we moved in together, I moved into his apartment and brought my things. When I left, I left everything. The only good thing about what he did that evening was that he smashed both my phone and my laptop. I know he did it to spite me, but the result was he spited himself. Had he not broken them, he could probably have quickly tracked me down. He would have found emails and text messages leading him to Cambridge.

I wonder what he's doing now. I wonder if he ever thinks about me and regrets how he behaved.

As I'd done so many times before, I wished it could have been different. I wished he had been different.

The doorbell interrupted my thoughts. When the furniture delivery guys had left, I spent the next few hours unpacking my bed and assembling everything. By the time I had finished, I was hot and sticky. After a quick shower, the first in my new bathroom, I headed back to Uncle Bill and Aunt Vickie's for dinner. Aunt Vickie had convinced me to stay there while I set up my apartment. I guess it took little to convince me; it was definitely easier. I'd still not done any grocery shopping, and I needed to buy a coffee pot before I moved in. I'd be glad when I started work and could pay Uncle Bill back for everything. Once again, I thought about how lucky I was. *So many women didn't have anyone to turn to like Grace and I have. Thank goodness for Caitlin and her Escape Route.*

As I stepped out and locked my front door, a young couple came in, heading to the main house. They paused and then came over and introduced themselves.

"Hi, I'm Gina, and this is my husband, Kyle."

"I'm Sally. Nice to meet you." We shook hands.

"I see you got the separate unit, lucky you! We're in the basement, actually it's really nice because it opens into the backyard. And we've a separate entrance."

"Oh, yes. I got this unit because I was the first to view the place and got my pick. But I did like your unit, too. It would have been my second choice. Lovely to have direct access to the backyard."

"We just got married last month. We moved here from Cincinnati for Kyle's work. He's a doctor."

"It's lovely to meet you both. I hope to see you around."

I watched them walk towards the basement entrance, arms around each other, and felt a pang of jealousy.

That's what I want. Someone to put his arm around me. Someone to grow old with.

~~

I worked through my list over the next week. Each day, I spent a few hours at the apartment. I made up the bed and added a nightstand and lamp to my shopping list. I put the table and chairs together and set them up in the dining area. Finally, I assembled the couch.

Aunt Vickie and Uncle Bill turned up with a beautiful flat screen TV as a housewarming gift, so I struck that off my list.

I showed Uncle Bill the apartment and I could see it impressed him. He particularly liked the small, private patio out back. He stood out there for a few seconds, looking around.

"You don't have a yard, but you could put a few planters around here and make it really nice. And it's very private."

Aunt Vickie smiled at him. "You love your gardening."

I'd also been to the grocery store and completely stocked my pantry, fridge, and freezer. Bought household cleaners and, of course, a coffee pot. I'd agreed with Aunt Vickie that I'd do my laundry at their place for the foreseeable future. They were so close, and my apartment didn't really have a suitable place for a washer and dryer, even if I were prepared to buy one and add to what I already owed them.

"You can come over every Sunday morning, do your laundry and have brunch while you're waiting for it," she said, with a satisfied look. I realized she was happy that they would continue to see me regularly. I would have visited regularly anyway, even if I didn't need to use their washer and dryer.

Finally, I went clothes shopping for work, then texted Pat with my new address. I was ready for the next chapter. There was still the last item on my list. I planned to do that the following weekend after I got myself a new laptop, and then it would be time to start a new list.

CHAPTER NINE

My first day of work was not easy. Mainly because I was so stressed. It had been over six months since I'd worked a normal job and even in that short time, so much had changed. I hoped I was ready for it. I spent the day meeting people, doing the usual 'first day' ritual. Lunch with the boss and my co-workers. Finally, I spent the last few hours with what the bank called my mentor. A co-worker assigned to help bring me up to speed. Amanda.

Amanda had been working at the bank in this branch for over a year. She started as a teller and she was still a teller, but with the title of head teller. She told me she was studying for her finance degree at night in order to get a further promotion.

I was to sit with Amanda for the full week; watch, listen and ask questions. Even though I had experience working as a teller and an assistant manager, sitting with Amanda for an entire week would help me get back into the swing of work. Malcolm's verbal and physical abuse had significantly damaged my confidence. I began to fully understand the importance of those months of therapy. I also appreciated the value studying for the financial consultant certification had, as Rick had promised, it bolstered my confidence.

The obligatory welcome lunch turned out to be an excellent opportunity to get a feel for the pecking order outside of the obvious office structure. It was a large group, ten of us, to be exact. As they showed us to our table, Amanda took charge of the seating arrangements. I realized she was very determined that she would sit beside Mark.

"Mark, you sit at the head of the table, here," she said. "Sally, as it's your welcome lunch, you sit there beside Mark. I'll sit on his other side, opposite you, as I'm to be your mentor." That was when she sat down and let everyone else decide where they were sitting.

At first, I assumed this to be a political move, as she considered herself more senior than everyone, except the assistant manager Leonard. He had not accompanied us. He and two others remained as the lunch hour staff. As lunch progressed, I suspected there was more to it than office politics. Amanda worked hard to hog Mark's attention, and I felt she was coming close to inappropriate flirting. I wondered if that was because she had a romantic interest in him, or if she thought it would help her get a promotion. I was pretty sure that if there was something between them, she would have been a lot more discreet in her behavior. Besides, he looked decidedly uncomfortable most of the time. Particularly whenever he tried to speak to me, and she interrupted. I had to work hard to not laugh at how blatant she was, though to be fair, I could understand her interest. He was a good-looking guy, and he was not wearing a wedding ring. I tried to avoid the uncomfortable battle to have a conversation with him by turning to Betty, a loan consultant, seated on my right. Towards the end of lunch, Amanda got up to go to the restroom and Mark turned to me.

"Great to have you join us, Sally. Do you think you can settle back into a teller role after having been an AM?"

"I'm sure I'll be quite happy. Thanks Mark. I need to get back into things slowly after six months away from it."

"Six months?" Betty said. "Were you sick or off on a trek around the world?"

"Actually, a small part was because of injury, but no, I moved from Texas, and I took time off to get my financial consultant certification."

"Oh, congratulations!"

"What's that?" Amanda said, as she sat down again.

"Sally took time off to get her FC certification. And did you know she used to be an assistant manager in a previous job?" It was clear from the glint in Betty's eyes as she said this that she was deliberately trying to irritate Amanda.

The look Amanda gave me was anything but congratulatory, but she congratulated me, although her voice sounded just as acidic as the look on her face.

"Studying at night and working during the day is the way most of us have to do it," she said.

I was already looking forward to next week and the end of my training sessions with her.

~~

That first week went by fast, despite having to sit each day with Amanda. I could feel the resentment coming off her like static electricity. I also noticed several occasions where she appeared to be deliberately giving me misinformation. The first couple of times, I repeated the faulty information loudly enough for the other tellers to hear. I asked her if I understood her instructions correctly. She quickly clarified and tried to make it sound like I was not very bright, that I had picked it up wrong. After that, I just kept quiet and pretty much ignored her. I knew the job as well, or better than she did. I didn't need training.

Friday evening finally came around. They'd given me my schedule for the following week, and my station was set up as I wanted it.

"Anyone going for a drink after work?" Betty called out as security locked the doors.

"Not me, thanks. I'm meeting family tonight," I said, grabbing my bag and heading for the door. "Good night, all. See you Monday."

I had driven to work that morning, partly because there was rain forecast and partly because I was way too tired to walk. I was glad I had. The rain was coming down steadily as I headed to Uncle Bill's and Aunt Vickie's.

Before I even opened the front door, I could hear yelping from inside. I rushed in to see what was making such a noise—and why? Uncle Bill was sitting on the couch with what looked like a ball of golden fluff. It was squirming and yelping. A puppy! I'd never known them to own a dog before. Whatever possessed them to get one now. Squatting down on the floor beside them, I held my hand out to the little animal.

"Here. She's yours. You take her." Uncle Bill thrust her into my arms. I sat down suddenly with the puppy alternately jumping, licking, and turning around in circles as she caught sight of her long tail waving furiously.

"Mine? Are you serious?"

Aunt Vickie came in from the kitchen wiping her hands on her apron and smiling. "We decided it would be good company for you, living on your own for the first time in a while."

"She's gorgeous. I just love her already." I swallowed the lump in my throat and blinked as I picked up the boisterous ball of fur. "What's her name?"

"She's your dog Sal. You give her a name," Uncle Bill said.

I thought for just a few seconds. "Hawn!"

"Hawn? What sort of name is that?"

"Well, Goldie is the obvious name, but it's too obvious."

Uncle Bill and Aunt Vickie looked at me as though I were crazy. Then they both got it at the same time.

Aunt Vickie laughed as she headed back into the kitchen.

Uncle Bill followed her.

"Come on, Hawn, let's go," I said to the puppy as I stood up and joined them, with Hawn jumping around my feet.

There was a large crate in one corner. Inside was a comfortable-looking cushion and a small bowl of water.

"We got you a crate big enough to last her for a while," Uncle Bill said, pointing to it.

"Thank you so much." I hugged them both as Hawn wandered into her crate and noisily lapped from the water bowl there before flopping down on the cushion.

After dinner, Uncle Bill loaded the crate, with Hawn inside it, into the back of Aunt Vickie's SUV, and drove to my apartment. There was no way it would fit in my car. I helped him carry it into my kitchen and as soon as he left, I let Hawn out to investigate her new home. Of course, the first thing she did was pee on the kitchen floor, before I had time to put out the pads Uncle Bill had given me.

First thing tomorrow morning, I'll sign up for dog training. I thought as I cleaned up.

~~

I arrived at the bank early, before anyone else, and I busied myself making coffee. That was the first thing I had learned. Whoever gets there first makes the coffee. After that, whoever takes the last cup, makes another pot.

Mark came into the kitchen just as I was pouring my first cup.

"Ah. I see you made the coffee. Great, thanks," he said, getting himself a mug and filling it. "You make excellent coffee." He sipped the steaming liquid.

I don't know how he could taste anything—it was so hot. "I just followed the instructions," I said, smiling as I headed to my station to get set up, ready for my first day of real work. He followed me out and stood awkwardly behind the counter for a few minutes before heading to his office. I'm not sure if he felt he should make conversation, but couldn't think of anything to say, or if he expected me to say something. Either way, it was an uncomfortable silence, and I was glad when he left.

"Good morning, Sally." Betty hustled past to get coffee before we opened to the public. "How was your weekend?"

Clearly, she didn't actually want a detailed response because she didn't stop. When she returned with her coffee, she sat down at the station to my right.

"Sorry, how was your weekend?" She smiled.

"Great thanks. My uncle gave me a puppy, a golden retriever. I spent most of the weekend working with her. We signed up for training at the local pet store."

"Oh, how lovely? I love golden retrievers. What did you call her? Goldie?"

I shook my head. "Hawn."

Betty paused for only a second before bursting out laughing. "Brilliant name," she said. "Talk to you later." She headed to her office, still chuckling.

I wondered how she would react if I told her about the rest of my weekend. And the two on-line dating sites I signed up for. There wasn't much to tell about it, really. I signed up yes; completed the profile questions, but nothing else. I'm not even sure what I expected. I really wanted to find a man I could love, one who loved me back. In my mind, I wanted what my parents had. I knew it was possible because I had seen it with my own eyes, with them, and with Uncle Bill and Aunt Vickie.

CHAPTER TEN

Online dating didn't turn out to be what I expected. I was expecting something like a more mature version of the first few months at college. Where all the guys looked like hunks and hours, sometimes days, of butterflies and excitement preceded every date. No, nothing like that.

Each evening, as soon as I got home from work, I took Hawn out for a long walk. Once her energy levels had reduced, we spent some time working on the training exercises the pet store trainer had given us. After that I got online and checked for any contact from men. After a full week and my in-box was still empty, I started searching for guys in my area, and getting the courage to reach out to a few of them. It took a couple of weeks, but finally I began chatting with one guy, and we arranged to meet.

The first thing I realized almost immediately was that online profiles are rarely honest. Profile photos were often at least ten years old, if not older, depicting slim men with a full head of hair, and often a fancy car in the background. I had no doubt most of the women's profiles were equally fictitious.

That first date I was inexperienced enough to allow the man, Rod, to pick me up from my home. I later realized what a mistake that could be. Fortunately, he was harmless. However, he arrived in a small RV, which I found somewhat disconcerting.

I followed him to his vehicle, in his vapor trail of an assortment of well-aged colognes and aftershaves, a cocktail that was somewhat pungent, to say the least.

"I'm afraid I had to take the RV this evening. When I came out of the house, I discovered I had a flat on the car. I tried to change it, but the spare was also flat. I hope you don't mind." He leered at me as he opened the passenger door.

We went to a bar downtown and as our drinks were being served, I wondered why on earth I had agreed to meet this man.

What is wrong with me?

Just as I had that thought, he leaned across the table and kissed me on the cheek. The horror I felt must have shown on my face.

"Your profile said you're shy, so I thought that would be a good idea to break the ice and make you feel more comfortable," he said.

I was speechless and finished my drink in silence, refusing a second. I told him I needed to get home.

The next date was a guy called Peter. He made the unreliability of the profiles obvious. He declared himself to be an executive—he was a traveling sales agent. Cambridge (supposedly his home) was just another port. He lived in North Carolina and visited Cambridge twice a week. He clearly had not touched a female in years. At the bar, he found any excuse to brush against me. I edged my stool a little further away from him.

"Where did you get your nail polish? It's a fabulous color," he said, grabbing my hand.

I yanked my hand back and grasped my drink with both hands, without answering him. Of course, I was looking for a man to touch me, emotionally as well as physically. But not this man, and not without getting to know him first, and certainly not without some signal from me. Once again, I couldn't wait for the evening to end. At least this time, I had driven myself. I didn't see either of them again.

~~

Sam was also a mistake. In fact, he was the one who convinced me that online dating was not the answer. When I met Sam, he was on the rebound. He was totally obsessed with his ex-girlfriend, Anna. On our first date, he told me I could never live up to her. Even that didn't stop me from hoping. Apart from his obsession, he was fun. We shared a love of animals, though I must admit, Sam went a bit over the top. He collected every stray cat or dog he came across and brought them home. When I met him, he had four cats and three assorted dogs.

I enjoyed his company, and convinced myself that as our relationship developed, he would forget Anna—that is another lesson I needed to learn. If he tells you who he is, believe him.

On our second date, we went to a fancy restaurant close to the bank. As we were waiting for our table, Amanda came out with two women. When she saw me, she stopped and stared at Sam.

"Sally! Hello—Girls, this is Sally from work. Sally, these are my roommates. Alice and Inga." She stood there looking from me to Sam.

"Oh. Hi Amanda. This's Sam."

I shook hands with Alice and Inga while Amanda grabbed Sam's hand and started firing questions at him—where he worked and where he lived. Luckily, at that moment our table was called, and we escaped.

I realized things would not work out between us on our fourth date. We were supposed to be going out for dinner. As the restaurant was close to where he lived, he suggested I meet him at his house, and we go from there. I took that to be a good sign.

When I knocked on his front door, he yelled, "the door's not locked, come on in."

I walked into his kitchen to find him on his knees on the floor, sorting through a pile of trash. There were two large black trash bags to one side.

"Look at all this," he said. "There's so much information here." He held up what looked like a cell phone bill.

"What is it? Have you lost something?" I couldn't figure out why he would sift through his trash.

"No! This is Anna's trash! I was watching her house earlier when I saw her putting it out." He was talking fast and when he looked at me, his eyes were wide, and a bit scary. "As soon as she went inside, I grabbed them. Now I can find out who she's calling. A phone bill, and see here, a gas card bill! I can tell where she's going by where she filled up. It's all here!" He sat back on his heels and took a deep breath before diving back into the assorted rotting vegetables, coffee grounds, and paperwork.

"Wait—you were watching her house?"

"Yes, I photograph any cars that stop there so I can look up the plate numbers."

"You take pictures of her visitors?"

"Yeah, I have a zoom lens, so it's okay. They don't see me."

"You have a zoom lens—and you took her trash!"

"Great idea, right?"

I stood there for a second, trying to sort it out in my head.

Then he said something that had me running. "One thing that is bothering me is that I haven't been able to find any feminine hygiene items." He dived into the trash again.

"Sam—" he looked up and stopped what he was doing for a second. I shook my head. "Goodbye." I almost ran out of the house. I could hear him calling my name as I slammed his front door, jumped into my car and fled home.

That night, I deleted my online accounts for both websites I'd signed up on. Then I took a long, hot shower. I felt dirty. I felt stupid. But most of all, I felt relief that I had found out before things got more serious.

After I deleted my accounts, I got up from my desk and as I moved to sit on the couch, Hawn jumped up beside me and rested her head on my lap.

"Looks like it's just you and me, Hawn." I said, fondling her ears. "Dating men I work with is out. Online dating is a disaster. I'm not sure how I can meet a man like my dad or Uncle Bill. Maybe I'll ask Aunt Vickie how they met."

~~

I spent most of the weekend working with Hawn. On Sunday morning, we walked to Uncle Bill and Aunt Vickie's. Ever since I moved into my apartment, I did my laundry there. I brought it in a small roller bag, and we had Sunday brunch together. We sat on the back patio drinking mimosas, while we watched Hawn chasing butterflies among the flower beds. When I'd answered all their usual questions about work and Hawn's training progress. I took a deep breath.

"Aunt Vickie, do you know how my parents met?"

She looked at me with surprise. "I thought you knew. They were high school sweethearts. They lost touch for years when they went off to different colleges. Then they met again when they were working on the academic staff in UT. It was very romantic."

"So, they actually met at work?"

"Well, they met at school, but yes, they got back together after they met at work. Why?"

"I dunno. I just thought—after Malcolm—it's a bad idea to date someone you work with."

"My dear, how Malcolm behaved had nothing to do with the fact that you worked together. He was just bad."

"Okay, so how did you and Uncle Bill meet?"

"Almost the same story." Aunt Vickie grinned. "We met at Harvard, but I wasn't on the staff. I was a student in one of his classes."

"Isn't there some sort of rule about professors dating students?"

"We didn't date while I was in his class. In fact, he waited until graduation day to ask me out. I didn't even know he was interested in me before that."

None of that helps me. Unless I go back to college—and that's not going to happen. I guess I missed my chance.

~~

Next morning, I was once again the first to arrive at the office. As I was making the coffee, Amanda came into the kitchen.

"Oh, hey Sally." It was the first time she had been in any way friendly and it took me by surprise.

"Hi Amanda." I finished up with the coffee and sat down to wait for it to percolate.

"Thanks for fixing the coffee again," she said, sitting down beside me. "Funny running into you and—Sam was his name, right?"

I just nodded, wondering what she was after.

"It's funny, you know. I really thought that you had a thing for Mark." Her laugh sounded a little forced.

"For Mark—our manager? Oh no, I think it's a bad idea to date someone you work with," I said.

"Not at all. I don't think that's a problem at all. Where else would you meet someone with the same interests as you?"

Suddenly, I realized what was going on. I was right. Amanda had a thing for Mark, and she saw me as competition. Now that she thought I was otherwise engaged, she was happy to be friendly.

Who needs friends like that? On the other hand, I don't want to make an enemy of her.

That evening, I left the building at the same time as Amanda and started walking towards my apartment.

"Oh. I thought Sam was here to pick you up?" Amanda said, looking around. "I'm sure I saw him at the corner waiting."

"Sam? No, why on earth would he be here? You must be mistaken."

"I'm sure it was him. I just assumed he was waiting for you. Perhaps he was just taking photos."

"Taking photos?" I looked around. "Are you sure?"

"Yeah, he had a fancy camera with a zoom lens."

"Zoom lens?" I realized I probably sounded a bit stupid. "No, I wasn't expecting him. Good night, Amanda. See you in the morning."

She gave me an odd look. I hurried off, making a mental note to add buying a cross shredder to my list. At least if it was Sam, and if he was now stalking me—and if he took my trash, it wouldn't give him any information.

CHAPTER ELEVEN

I'd been working at the bank for over six weeks when Betty came over to me and said that Mark would like to see me in his office. I sat staring at her without moving.

"I think he wants to see you now," she said.

"Oh no, did I do something wrong?" That was my first thought. I hadn't intended to say it out loud, it just came out.

"I don't think so," Betty said. "He didn't seem upset. Probably just wants to do a six-week review to see how you're getting on."

As I stood up, I saw Amanda giving me an icy stare. She quickly looked away when she caught me looking at her.

"Come in Sally," Mark said when I knocked on his office door. It was already open. "Take a seat." He pointed to the chair across from him. Then he got up and closed the door after me. "How are things going?" he asked as he sat down again.

"Fine, thanks." As far as work was concerned, that was true.

"Good, good." His chair creaked slightly as he leaned back. He sat forward again and shuffled some papers on his desk before taking a deep breath. He looked at me with a strange look on his face. A cross between fear and determination.

"What's up? Have I done something wrong?"

"Oh no, definitely not. You are clearly way overqualified for the job, and you are very good at what you do. No, it's just—" the chair creaked again, "—Len has given notice, Leonard, my AM; and I was wondering if you would be prepared to consider stepping into that role? I would like to put your name forward?" He hesitated before continuing, "I think the job perfectly suits you and I would love it if you would consider it. We could work very well together, I believe."

I said nothing. I was thinking about how Amanda would take it.

"What's the problem? You don't look too pleased with the idea."

"Actually, I'm not sure if I'm ready to step back into that role again, but I was wondering how Amanda would react. After all, she really is in line for it."

"Hmm—" Mark studied the tips of his fingers, which were currently held as though he were praying. "I guess you're right that she probably believes she should be in line for it. But I doubt head office would even consider her. I know she's working on her degree, but she doesn't have it yet and I don't believe she has the trust of her colleagues."

That comment surprised me. I didn't think Mark was aware of the undercurrents of tension Amanda caused. I started to wonder if perhaps he was aware of her fixation with him. If he was, that would definitely go against her, too.

"To address your other concern, I believe you're ready and able for the position. I would really like it if you were also willing. Take a few days to think about it. Let's see, today is Thursday. How about we set up a time on Monday? You can give me your decision then?"

"Okay," I said, standing up to leave.

"Thanks Sally. I'll block off time on my calendar and send you a notification." He turned to his computer as I left and went back to my station.

"Everything okay?" Amanda said, as I sat down.

"Oh yeah, just a six-week review, as Betty said."

Towards the end of the day, as everyone was packing up, I went looking for Betty. I found her in the kitchen.

"Hey Betty, do you have time to go for a drink after work? I wanted to get your opinion on something."

"Absolutely, I would love to. Let me go shut down my computer and I'll be with you."

"Let's just let Amanda go before we do. I would rather she didn't join us."

"I hear you." Betty grinned.

Thirty minutes later, we were sitting at a corner table in the local bar. Each with a glass of sparkling wine.

"So, what's up? Something to do with your chat with Mark earlier?"

"Yes. Thing is, not sure if this is confidential, so please keep it to yourself." I waited for her response. She smiled and nodded. "Leonard is leaving and—"

"Mark wants you to be AM? Brilliant!"

"Really? You think it would work? I mean, I know Amanda's going to be pissed, but do you think everyone else would be cool with it? And it isn't for sure yet anyway."

"Huh. Amanda will be pissed no matter what. She thinks she's better than everyone else; she thinks she's better than she is. There's no way she would make AM, and if she did, I think we would all leave—I know I would. We know you've been an AM before and to be honest, most of us wonder why you took a job as a teller in the first place."

"Well, that makes me feel better about it. I've a meeting with Mark on Monday to let him know my decision."

Betty shook her head slowly. "You mean you didn't accept yet!?"

"Like I said, it isn't for sure yet. If I agree, then Mark has to put my name forward and head office will decide. I wanted to think about it and talk to my uncle first. Then I thought it might be a good idea to ask your opinion."

"Thank you. I take that as a compliment. I'll not say a word, I promise." She raised her glass to me, and I raised mine and touched it against hers before taking a long drink. I started to feel better about the idea.

It was difficult to get through Friday at work. Betty kept giving me knowing looks, and I felt sure Amanda was being even more obvious in her flirting; I have to admit she was good at staying just within proprietary behavior, but only just barely. I was glad that I had the weekend to gather my thoughts and talk to Uncle Bill and Aunt Vickie.

~~

I spent Saturday mulling over the pros and cons while working with Hawn. She was coming along really well and the trainer at the pet shop said she was very intelligent, and it was obvious I'd been putting a lot of work into her training. At least I was getting that right.

On Sunday morning, I took Hawn for a long walk. Then I picked up my laundry from home and we headed to Uncle Bill and Aunt Vickie's for our usual brunch.

"How's work going?" Aunt Vickie asked, as she did every week.

But she really wanted to know. She wasn't just being polite.

"Actually, I wanted to talk to y'all about that."

Uncle Bill laughed. "I guess you won't ever leave Texas behind—y'all!"

I smiled. "About work. The manager told me last week that the assistant manager was leaving, and he asked me if I would consider the position, if he put my name forward."

"I hope you said yes," Uncle Bill said, with no sign of laughter.

"I told him I would think about it. I'm scheduled to meet with him tomorrow morning to tell him my decision."

"What's to think about?" Aunt Vickie said. "You've done the job before. You are more than qualified, and they are lucky to have you, besides I'm sure he wouldn't have asked you if he didn't think you were capable."

"Why're you hesitant?" Uncle Bill said. While they are both equally supportive, he's a lot more practical, and I guess he could see I was having doubts. Why else would I want to discuss it with them?

"Well—back in Austin, when I did that job before, I felt I wasn't very good at it. I kept making stupid mistakes."

"Why? Let me guess, because Malcolm said so? The same guy who beat you up? Yeah, you mentioned that before." Uncle Bill said, sitting forward, his face flushed and his voice getting louder.

"Shush, Bill," Aunt Vickie said, putting a hand on his arm. "You'll wake the dog."

I glanced down at Hawn, curled up at my feet, and smiled.

"Yes. It was him."

"That was just a control tactic, and probably a whole lot of jealousy, too," Uncle Bill said more quietly. "He was just trying to undermine your self-confidence."

"That's what my therapist said. I just wanted to be sure you guys were in favor."

"Aye!" Uncle Bill said.

"Aye!" Aunt Vickie said.

"Thank you both. I love you." I blinked hard and smiled at them.

"And we love you too, my dear," Aunt Vickie said.

"You go into your manager in the morning and tell him yes," Uncle Bill said, leaning across and squeezing my hand.

CHAPTER TWELVE

Next morning, at ten, I closed my station and headed towards Mark's office. As I crossed the foyer of the bank, I could feel Amanda's eyes boring into my back. I passed Betty, and she winked at me. I knocked on Mark's open door and he immediately stood up.

"Come in Sally, close the door and take a seat."

As soon as I was sitting down, he sat down again and said, "What's the verdict? Can I put your name forward?"

I nodded. "Yes. And thank you for the vote of confidence."

"Great news!" Mark sat back in his chair, grinning. "You joined us at just the right time. Replacing Len would be very difficult if we didn't have such an ideal candidate already on staff." He looked at me for a second, his brows drawn together in a frown. "I know you're aware that you might have some push back from Amanda. She's very ambitious and has had her eye on the AM position for a while. To be perfectly honest, I would find it very difficult to work alongside her."

I said nothing; anything I was thinking was definitely not appropriate for the situation and best left unsaid.

"Okay. I'll advise head office. I don't expect them to have any objections. In fact, I'm fairly sure they'll be delighted to have such an easy transition. It's much easier to replace a teller than it is to replace an assistant manager. As soon as I have their approval, I'll announce it to the staff."

As I got up to go, he said, "no need to mention it; no need to say anything at the moment, especially about Len leaving."

I nodded and returned to my station, feeling Amanda's venomous stare all the way across the foyer. I kept my head down and avoided making eye contact with her. It would be difficult to explain why I might have had another review so soon after the last one. Fortunately, we got busy, and I spent the next hour dealing with a long line of customers. She had no opportunity to ask questions.

~~

The following day, I was once more summoned to Mark's office. Thankfully, Amanda was not at the counter. She was on an early lunch, so I didn't have to deal with that.

"Come in Sally, I just wanted to let you know that head office is delighted to offer you the position of AM as I expected. Naturally, there'll be an increase in your compensation. You'll receive official notification of all of that. I'll go ahead and set up an all staff meeting to make the announcement of Len's departure and your promotion."

"Oh—Oh, thanks Mark. I'll say nothing until then." I headed back to my station. Luckily, I immediately had a customer, so I didn't have time to think further about it.

It didn't surprise me, therefore, when Mark sent out a notice that there would be a staff meeting immediately after the bank closed that day. It was fairly normal to do that. If we had a staff meeting, it was after we close, officially our working hours extended beyond closing to the public. Staff meetings, on the other hand, were not very frequent, so there was a bit of a buzz as everyone wondered what it was about. Betty and I kept our heads down and avoided joining in the guessing game. Leonard remained in his office with the door shut.

Finally, the security guard locked the front door. Everyone closed up their stations. Shut down their computers and took care of end of day stuff before heading to the kitchen, the location Mark had set for the meeting.

The hum of chatter stopped as Mark and Leonard walked in. Mark started the meeting with the standard praise for the good work everyone was doing, then he paused for effect.

"I have some bad news and some good news," he said. "I'll start with the bad news and get that out of the way. Len, here, has handed in his resignation. Friday will be his last day."

There was the expected wave of "Oohs", "Ah's" and a few "Oh

no" exclamations. I noticed Amanda edging closer to where Mark was standing with a look of anticipation on her face.

"And I know we'll all miss Len, and naturally, we wish him all the very best in his next venture. The good news is that Sally has agreed to step up and take over the job of AM. That means we shouldn't miss a beat, as we already know and love Sally." He paused for the round of applause. "And of course, we also know that she has previous experience in this role, plus almost two months of working at this branch under her belt."

Another round of applause. I noticed Amanda wasn't joining in the clapping. In fact, if looks could kill, I would most definitely have collapsed on the floor, drawing my last breath. I caught Betty's eye, and it was all I could do to keep a straight face, because the face she was making in Amanda's direction was hilarious. Thank goodness I had her support. This would not be easy. It looked like everyone else was on my side. I would just have to work on winning Amanda over. My first major challenge as AM.

After Mark's announcement, Leonard said a few words. The standard stuff about missing us and how great we all were. Then Mark opened up the refrigerator, pulled a couple of bottles of sparkling wine out. Leonard set out champagne glasses from a carton under the table.

"And now we'll have a toast, to wish both Len and Sally the best of luck in their new ventures," Mark said, popping open one of the bottles.

I saw Betty coming towards me with her glass raised, then Amanda stepped in front of her and walked up to me.

"So. That's why you were in and out of Mark's office so much the past few days, I suppose?"

"Yes, I'm afraid it was a bit cloak and dagger, but he asked me not to say anything until we had cleared it through head office."

"Congratulations," Betty said, managing to squeeze around Amanda.

"Of course, people who can afford to take time off to get degrees and certifications get to be top of the list for promotion," Amanda said, turning away and heading towards Mark, and a refill for her glass.

"Oh dear. I wonder how we are going to get past this one. Just as she was beginning to get friendly," I said to Betty.

"I'm not sure anyone can get through to that girl. She has such a chip on her shoulder. Just don't start dating Mark or you will really be in the shit." Betty laughed. I did not! The idea horrified me. Not that he wasn't attractive, but I was still not sure that things went sour between me and Malcolm because we worked together. Besides, as Betty pointed out, Amanda already hated me enough. That might just push her over the edge. I guess, from her point of view, I had stolen her promotion. She just might get over that. If I also stole her crush, that would be unforgivable. Besides all that, I couldn't imagine Mark being interested in me.

CHAPTER THIRTEEN

The rest of the week was filled with meetings. Meetings with Leonard as he brought me up to speed; meetings with Mark, and meetings with both of them. I kept looking out the office windows, thinking how wiring Amanda up to the grid would save a lot of money on electricity, not just for the bank, but for the entire area. She was literally bristling. I could almost see sparks coming off her. I actually felt sorry for her. Particularly as her reaction was so obvious to everyone, any hope she might have had of impressing Mark was definitely gone that week.

During one of the earlier meetings I had with Mark, he told me they signed me up for a two-day conference in New York the following week.

"What's it for?"

"Mainly an introduction to the higher ups—for them to meet you, but it's also educational. You'll find it very useful. There'll be a number of sessions and all employees who've been promoted in the past quarter, from all branches, will attend. Is it a problem?"

"No problem. I'll need to arrange for someone to look after my dog, but that should be easy enough. I'm sure my aunt and uncle will take her."

"Great. Joan will take care of your travel and accommodation. You should receive details tomorrow."

That evening, as I was leaving the office, Amanda caught up with me.

"Meeting up with Sam again this evening?" She asked.

I shook my head. "No, I'm not, why?"

"Oh. I saw him hanging around outside earlier. He was peeping through the window. I just assumed he was looking for you."

"Are you sure it was him?"

"Oh yes, I went out and told him you were in a meeting. I asked him if I could give you a message. He said no, he was just passing by."

I felt like my hair was standing on end. I put a hand up to pat it into place. Amanda gave me an odd look.

"Are you okay? You look like you've seen a ghost."

"Yeah, I'm fine, thanks. Look, I'm not dating Sam anymore, so if you see him again, please don't talk to him about me."

"Oh. Okay." Amanda gave me another weird look, opened her mouth as if she was going to say something. Closed it again and shrugged as she walked off.

I hurried home, checking each corner and occasionally looking behind me to see if I spotted Sam. I finally had to accept he was definitely stalking me. At least I had bought a cross shredder and was using it to shred everything that would go through it.

~~

The two days of training in New York were fascinating and well worthwhile. If it had been the same for my promotion in my previous job, perhaps I would not have paid attention to Malcolm when he told me I couldn't do the job. The hotel was luxurious. As Mark had said, all the other attendees were just promoted to manager or assistant managers at other branches; or were new hires to one of those positions. It was useful to exchange ideas and doubts with them and discover that we all felt the same—nervous.

On the first day, one of the first events was photographs. They arranged us in various groups. The final one was all the new managers and assistant managers in a group. We were told this was for the bank newsletter that was about to go to press. At the end of the two days, I was ready to go home.

Uncle Bill met me at the airport with Hawn. He picked me up outside the arrivals so that he didn't have to leave her on her own in the truck. I'm not sure which of them appeared happier to see me. I guess Hawn, because Uncle Bill didn't jump up and down, but he did hug me twice when he met me and again when he dropped me off at home. He carried Hawn's crate into the apartment for me. As soon as he headed off, I spent twenty minutes making a fuss of her before unpacking and preparing for my first day on the job as assistant manager.

When I arrived at the office, as usual, I was the first there. I made the coffee and then headed to Leonard's—now my office. Before I even opened the door, I could see the balloons and streamers through the window. Someone, no doubt Betty, had decorated it and there was a congratulations card on my desk, signed by everyone. The card and a bowl of peony roses, my favorite flowers, sat side by side. I was glad no one else was around to see the tears, which I quickly wiped before setting my coffee mug on a coaster on the desk. Beside the card was the bank's quarterly newsletter, including the photo, the one taken on the first day, of all the newly promoted employees together at the conference. There I was, standing in the back row. Below the photo was a list of all the names and the branches where they were located.

My smile didn't last long as I suddenly realized that perhaps Malcolm could somehow see this. After all, he worked for a bank in Austin. He might still work there, or at some other bank. It was a bit of a stretch, but still a worry. I needed to contact Pat to find out if she knew where he was. I texted her. It would probably be too early in Austin to expect an immediate response, but I knew she would get back to me when she could. I spent the rest of the morning trying to get some work done while being interrupted every few minutes by someone dropping by to congratulate me. Even Amanda came by.

"All settled in, I see," she said, looking around. "It feels strange not to see Leonard in here. So, is your boyfriend excited about your promotion?"

I immediately understood that she was fishing to see if I was dating someone. She'd been more comfortable when she thought I was dating Sam; I guess she wanted to make sure that I would not be competition for Mark.

"After breaking up with Sam, I'm taking a break from dating." I said, trying to make her feel better. It seemed to work as she left my office, smiling.

My phone pinged, and I picked it up. Pat, great.

Pat: Got your text. Congratulations on your promotion. I'll check with Caitlin to find out what the situation is with Malcolm and will get back to you when I hear.

It wasn't until after I got home that Pat got back to me. I had just returned from walking Hawn when my phone rang.

"Sally? Hi. I thought it would be easier to talk than to text this."

"Thanks for getting back to me, Pat. What did Caitlin say?" I propped the phone under my chin while I filled Hawn's water bowl.

"Turns out that Malcolm has been in prison for the last six months. He broke into Caitlin's home and then, after she got a restraining order against him, he tried again. He only recently got released and, as expected, he couldn't regain his previous job at the bank or any other bank."

"Oh, no! That was my fault. I should never have called to her home. Did he hurt her?"

"No, she called the police when he started banging on her door. They arrived just as he broke the door down."

"Thank goodness, and thanks for checking. I was afraid that he might see the newsletter and know exactly where I am."

"No, I think you're safe enough. He's currently working with some cleaning service company."

We continued chatting for a few minutes before hanging up. At least I didn't have to worry about Malcolm, as well as Sam. I decided it would probably be a good idea to get advice on what to do about stalkers. I fired up my laptop and went into the kitchen to get something to eat.

When I sat down again and logged in, I did a few Google searches on how to deal with stalkers. Added a few URLs to my favorites list to follow up and take some recommended action. Just not tonight—it had been a long day, and I was ready to just relax.

CHAPTER FOURTEEN

Report stalkers to the police.
That was the top of the list of recommendations from my Google search. It wasn't the least attractive choice, but it was something I really didn't want to do. I guess I had a built-in aversion to going to the police because I could still hear Malcolm's threats in my head. If I ever went to the police about his violence, he said he would kill me. But this wasn't Malcolm, it was Sam. And it's not my imagination because I already knew he was stalking his ex-girlfriend. After all, that was why I stopped seeing him. But my search results also warned stalkers can be more prone to violence. Particularly those with whom you were personally involved. What is it about me that seems to attract these guys? I know all men are not like that. I saw how wonderful my father was, and Uncle Bill, too.

On Saturday morning, I took Hawn for a long walk and did some obedience training with her before heading to the local police station. When I walked in, a policewoman looked up from the counter that served as a reception desk and asked what she could do for me.

"I'm not sure. I understand that if I believe I'm being stalked, I should report it?"

"Absolutely, you should. Let me get someone to talk to you." She got up and disappeared around a partition. A few minutes later, a door at the end of the counter opened and an elderly policeman came out.

"Ms. Simms?"

I nodded. "Sally," I said.

"Okay, Sally, follow me." He led me down a corridor and into a small room with just a desk and a chair on either side. "Take a seat, please," he said, placing a tablet on the table in front of him and firing it up, ready to take notes.

He asked me a bunch of questions, starting with the obvious. Who did I think was stalking me? How did I know him and what made me think he was a stalker? As I answered his questions, he tapped away on the tablet.

Finally, he asked me if I believed Sam might be violent. Did I think I was in danger?

I thought for a minute before answering. "I really don't know. But I'm not a good judge where that's concerned. Right now, I just find it really creepy, especially considering I know what he was doing to his ex—I bought a cross shredder."

He smiled and said, "That's always a sensible thing, with so much identity theft going on." He stood up. "Okay Sally, I think I've got everything I need. Naturally, there's not really anything we can do, but now that we're aware of the situation, if you need us, we'll be there with no delay. Don't hesitate to call if you're at all worried."

The next thing suggested by my search was definitely the least attractive. Tell those people you are close to.

~~

On Sunday morning, I followed my usual schedule and arrived on time at Uncle Bill's. Then, after we'd eaten and were sitting on the deck relaxing, I told them.

"I have to tell you something," I said, waiting to make sure I had their attention. "A couple of months ago, I started dating a guy." Aunt Vickie sat up and studied me with a look of anticipation. Uncle Bill stared at me, frowning. "I only went out with him a few times. As soon as I discovered he was stalking his ex-girlfriend, I walked away."

"Good girl." Uncle Bill said, visibly relaxing.

"The problem is, it would appear that he is now stalking me. One evening, when I was with him, we bumped into a girl from work, at a restaurant, so she met him. Since then, she told me she has seen him hanging around the bank a few times and—"

"Perhaps he just had business there?" Aunt Vickie interrupted.

"No. The thing is, when he told me he was watching his ex, he mentioned he had bought a zoom lens and was taking photographs of anyone who visited her. Amanda said he had a camera with a zoom lens. Anyway, I bought a cross shredder, and I reported it to the local police. I just wanted you guys to be aware."

Uncle Bill nodded but said nothing.

"What did the police say? Can they do anything?" Aunt Vickie said.

"Not really. They took down all the information and said that if I was worried at any time to call and they would make it a priority. If he doesn't break the law, they can't do anything, and taking photos is not against the law."

"You have not been very lucky with men, that's for sure," Uncle Bill sighed. "Okay, you be sure to call us if you feel, in any way, in danger. Is there anything else we can do?"

"Well, my Google search mentioned making sure to have an alarm system on your home and a web cam of some sort. I'm going to ask my landlord if I can get a video doorbell and an alarm system installed."

"Great idea! Let me know if you need help with that. I can ask around at the college for someone to do that for you."

As I got up to leave, Uncle Bill said, "You should probably let your manager know this creep is hanging around the bank. Just as a precaution."

The idea of talking to Mark about it horrified me. "Oh no, I'm sure that isn't necessary."

"Well, think about it, dear. What if he talked to your manager when you were not there? He could get information from him or even bad mouth you to him."

"Oh Bill, what a terrible thought!" Aunt Vickie said.

"Well, if he's evil enough to stalk his ex-girlfriend while dating Sally, and then stalk Sally after they break up, I think he's capable of anything. Better to cover all the possible angles."

"I guess you're right. I know my manager wouldn't tell him anything. But anyone who steals someone's trash and empties it out on their kitchen floor is definitely capable of anything," I said.

"He did that? No wonder you bought a cross shredder," Aunt Vickie said.

They both hugged me a little closer before I left.

~~

On Monday morning, I scheduled a meeting with Mark. His calendar looked clear for the first half of the morning, so I slotted thirty minutes in at nine thirty. I was not looking forward to that, but Uncle Bill was right; it made sense.

At nine twenty-five, Mark came into my office, closed the door and sat down.

"Oh. I didn't mean for you to come in here." I was a bit embarrassed to be on what I considered to be the control side of the desk.

"No problem. What's on your mind? Hopefully, you're not rethinking the position?" he said, looking worried.

"No, no. Nothing like that."

"Good. Glad to hear that. So, what can I do for you?"

"Well—this is a bit awkward—I'm not sure how to start."

"Just spit it out and see what happens. That's always my motto."

I took a deep breath and explained the situation with Sam.

"As he'd been seen a few times, hanging around the bank, I felt it was best to let you know about it."

"Of course! That's terrible, I'm glad you thought to tell me. Did you report him to the police?"

"Yes, I did that last Saturday. I also told my uncle and aunt, and they suggested telling you."

"And you're sure that he's stalking you?"

"I'm afraid there's no doubt. You see, we split up because I discovered he was stalking his ex. Amanda—she met him once, so she knew who he was—spotted him a couple of times. He was hanging around outside with a camera and zoom lens."

Mark's expression was almost comical. "A zoom lens! The guy must have a screw loose."

"Yes, that's what's worrying about it."

"Thanks for letting me know. I'll be sure to watch out for him. Meanwhile, if you need anything at all, let me know. Here, let's exchange personal phone numbers just in case." He pulled out his phone and looked at me expectantly.

I gave him my number, and he tapped on his screen. "Okay, just sent you a text," he said as my phone pinged.

"Thank you." I didn't know what else to say. I felt uncomfortable, but like he said, it might be useful. Hopefully, I wouldn't ever need to use it.

For the next few weeks, I didn't leave the bank in the evening without first checking to make sure Sam was nowhere in sight. I finally started to relax and thought that perhaps he had lost interest or found another girl to stalk.

During those weeks, I arranged with the landlord to install an alarm system, and Uncle Bill got a couple of young students from the Computer Science department to come by. They installed a video doorbell and a security camera on the outer wall. They angled it to view the area to the side of the front door. All of that made me feel a lot more secure as I settled into the AM job.

My neighbors, Kyle and Gina, saw the camera going in and stopped to chat.

"That's a great idea," Kyle said.

"Yeah. I also got a video doorbell."

"Oh cool. We must look into getting one of those."

It wasn't long before another incident shattered my sense of security.

I stepped out of the bank one evening, just as a battered old camper truck pulled away from the curb across the street. It was out of sight around a corner before I could get a good look, but the driver looked just like Malcolm. My heart was beating so fast I thought I was going to faint. I just stood there, staring at the space where the camper had been. Perhaps I was getting paranoid. Maybe I needed to go back to therapy. First Sam and now Malcolm.

CHAPTER FIFTEEN

As soon as I got home from work, I called and made an appointment with my therapist. After all, even if I was not imagining things, I was clearly stressed, and I knew from experience, therapy is good no matter what.

The following day, as I was leaving the bank, I noticed the same camper parked across the road. I couldn't see anyone in the cab, but it made me feel uncomfortable that it was there at all. What if it was Malcolm? How did he find me? Did he see that bank newsletter? These and a stream of other questions ran through my mind as I almost ran home. What I wanted to do was lock the door and hide, but what I had to do was take Hawn for a walk and go through obedience training with her.

~ ~

Two hours later, when I turned the corner into my street, I saw the camper again. This time it was outside my apartment! My legs were like jelly. I wanted to turn and run. I didn't. As I approached the vehicle, the door opened, and yes, it was Malcolm. I realized I was not paranoid, but that knowledge did nothing to make me feel better. He climbed out and just stood there.

"What the hell are you doing here? And how did you know where I was?"

"Look Sally, I just wanted to talk to you. To tell you how sorry I am for all the pain I caused you. I wanted to let you know that I've been attending anger management and I'm no longer the same person as I was back then." The words came out in a rush, but he didn't move.

I was furious. Furious with myself because those old feelings stirred, and I so badly wanted to believe him. I still loved him and, worse, I felt sorry for him.

"How do you expect me to believe that?"

"I don't. If you tell me to leave and never come near you again, I'll do that. But I love you and I wanted to see if you would just give me one more chance?" He bent down to pat Hawn, who was sniffing around his feet and wagging her tail invitingly. She had learned not to jump and was showing great restraint.

"How did you know where I was?" I repeated.

"The company I work for—worked for—cleaned a lot of the banks in Austin. I found this in a waste bin in one of them." He pulled a crumpled copy of the bank newsletter out of his pocket. "I spotted you in the picture immediately."

Shit. I should have known. I didn't say that out loud. There was no knowing what would set him off.

"Did you drive here from Texas in that thing?" I said, pointing to the camper.

"Yes, I don't need a motel. I can sleep in it. And I would drive to the moon to see you, Sally."

"Well, go get back in it and leave me alone." I rushed into the apartment and closed the door.

I paced around the kitchen, trying to sort out my feelings. Trying to figure out what to do.

I couldn't go through that again, could I? It would be stupid to trust him. But what if he has changed? I would give up a chance at happiness. The first few weeks we dated, when we first met, were magical. I wanted that back again. But I never wanted to be a victim again. I peeped out the window. The camper was still there, but there was no sign of Malcolm.

~~

When I left for work the next morning, the camper was gone. I was furious with myself for being disappointed. It was the right decision. I'd told him to go, and he had gone. But that might mean he'd changed. He would never have just gone before. He would've been angry and, at the very least, he would've argued, even tried to bully me into letting him stay. Perhaps he has changed. And now he'd gone.

I spent the entire day at work, bouncing between feeling proud for telling him to go, and feeling guilty and miserable that he'd gone. It was a relief when it was time to go home. I kept hoping that perhaps he was back. He wasn't.

As I turned into my driveway after Hawn's walk, my heart lifted. The camper was parked in the driveway and Malcolm was standing on my doorstep with an enormous bunch of flowers. My eyes misted. I had to blink hard; it was an effort to avoid smiling.

"These are for you. I know I was terrible about not giving flowers to you before."

"Thank you. They're lovely." I said, trying not to sound too pleased.

"Okay, I guess I'll go. I need to find somewhere to eat." He turned towards the camper.

"I was about to make something. Why don't you come in and we can talk?"

Common sense told me not to trust him, but I didn't listen.

"Nice place you have here." Malcolm said, sitting at the breakfast bar in the kitchen.

I took care of Hawn's water and then started preparing dinner.

"Obviously, I didn't expect you, so you'll just have to make do with a salad. That's all I have." I knew salad was not his favorite meal, but it was what I'd planned.

"Salad is fine with me, thanks."

I studied him for a second to see if he was being sarcastic. He would have been in a foul humor all evening if I'd fed him salad for dinner when we were together before. There was no sign of sarcasm and no hint of anger. Perhaps he had changed.

Over dinner, Malcolm told me about his time in prison and the therapy he went through, including anger management.

"I don't ever expect you to forgive me." He said, holding both my hands in his, tears in his eyes. "I just hope you'll give me the opportunity to prove I've changed."

At that moment, I would've agreed to anything. I thought back to that evening. Hammering on Caitlin's back door. The pain in my heart was almost worse than the pain in my body. I'd promised myself that day to never allow myself to be in such a situation again. But what if he has changed? What if the anger management really worked?

I took a deep breath. "Malcolm—" I paused, trying to find the right words. "—even now, I'm on edge. Afraid to anger you."

"I'm so sorry, Sal. I really am. Please trust that I won't ever hurt you again. No matter what you decide."

We talked around the subject and eventually agreed that we would try again. He would sleep in his camper. I agreed he could leave it parked outside the apartment. I had two parking spots assigned to my apartment.

He looked so happy when he hugged me as he left. I felt a little better about the decision. I was not looking forward to telling Aunt Vickie and Uncle Bill. Or my therapist. I decided to cancel the therapy appointment. One less thing to worry about. Or perhaps I was afraid to disappoint Rick.

CHAPTER SIXTEEN

For the next few days, I saw very little of Malcolm. I wasn't sure if he was in the camper when I left for work in the morning, and most evenings it was gone when I got home from work, but back again by the time I returned from walking Hawn.

It was a good sign. The old Malcolm would have been at my door every minute, constantly begging to be taken back. Trying to make me feel guilty or bully me into giving in. The new Malcolm was different. Each evening, he came in for dinner, helped with clearing up after dinner. Thanked me and left.

Finally, on Thursday evening, I decided if I was serious about giving him a chance, before I did anything else, I needed to talk to Uncle Bill and Aunt Vickie about it. Obviously, they would not be happy.

~~

The following morning, as soon as I got into the office, I texted Aunt Vickie and suggested we meet for lunch. I decided it would be easier to tell her on her own and let her deal with telling Uncle Bill. She responded almost immediately, and we agreed to meet at a restaurant around the corner from the bank.

I had a hard time concentrating on work. I kept going over in my head how I would explain about Malcolm to Aunt Vickie. As the clock ticked towards lunchtime, I questioned my sanity. I felt it was only fair to give him a chance to prove that he had changed; but what if he hadn't? I was fairly sure Aunt Vickie would not agree with my decision, but I was equally sure she would support me no matter what. I just hoped that she could convince Uncle Bill.

Just in case I had a last-minute delay leaving the office, I slipped out a little early. I got to the restaurant fifteen minutes before Aunt Vickie. As the weather was perfect, I sat at one of the outdoor tables. A row of flowering plants separated the seating area from the sidewalk. I felt it might be a little more private than inside. The server brought me two menus just as Aunt Vickie arrived. She spotted me immediately and joined me.

"This is lovely," she said.

"The weather's so nice. I hope you don't mind sitting outside?"

"Oh, no. It's perfect."

We both studied the menu in silence, ordered, and when the server left, she looked at me expectantly. The awkward silence became too much for her.

"Well, dear?"

"You know me too well. Of course, I've something I need to talk to you about." I sighed. "I'm not sure where to start."

"Just start at the beginning, dear."

"Okay. Malcolm turned up."

"What!? Here!? Where is he?" She looked around as if expecting him to materialize.

I explained to her how he'd shown up and that he'd completed anger management.

"I hope you told him to leave you alone?"

"Yes, I did. And he left."

"Good."

"But then he came back with flowers. I just couldn't turn him away, Aunt Vickie. I still love him, and I believe him when he says he'll never hurt me again. Anger management works for so many people. It's therapy, after all. He told me all about it."

The look on her face was a mixture of fear, disbelief, and despair. "You can't really believe that, Sally?"

"I want to believe it. I feel I should at least give him a chance. He drove here from Texas, in a battered old camper, just to apologize. He said he would turn around and go back. Leave me alone. If I couldn't give him another chance." I tried to keep my voice from breaking; tried to stop the tears that were threatening to flow. "Please, Aunt Vickie, do you think you could convince Uncle Bill to meet him and try to forgive him?"

Aunt Vickie pulled a pack of tissues out of her purse and handed me one, as she dabbed at her eyes with another. Just then, our lunch was served. We both moved our salad around our plates with our forks, saying nothing for a few minutes.

"Of course, you're right," Aunt Vickie said. "We should give the boy a chance to prove that he has changed. But I don't know how we can trust him again after what he did to you. This is so difficult."

"He's going to live in his camper, and we have agreed to take it slowly." I took a sip of my sparkling water before continuing. "The thing is—I couldn't do this behind your backs. I need for you both to agree. Perhaps if I bring him on Sunday? You can meet him and decide then?"

Aunt Vickie tried to smile. She failed. It's not an easy thing to do with tears glistening on her cheeks and her eyebrows furrowed. "I'll talk to your Uncle Bill. Though I'm not looking forward to that conversation."

"Thank you! I know I should do it myself, but it was difficult enough for me to tell you."

This time she smiled, a small watery smile, but a smile.

As we left the restaurant, Aunt Vickie promised to call me that evening to let me know Uncle Bill's reaction.

~~

I had a hard time keeping my mind on my work that afternoon. I was relieved when it was finally time to head home. Malcolm's camper was gone. He had mentioned that he was going to look for work.

As I walked Hawn, I kept checking my phone in case I'd missed a call from Aunt Vickie. When I got home, there was still no sign of Malcolm. I was just as glad, because I wanted to have an answer from Uncle Bill before I spoke to him again.

It wasn't until I'd just finished dinner that my phone finally rang. I snatched at it so fast I almost knocked it off the table.

"Hello, Aunt Vickie?"

"Hi Sal, sorry for the delay, but your uncle and I had a lot to talk about. Let me put you on to him."

"Sally?"

"Hi, Uncle Bill." My voice came out in a squeak.

"Sally? Are you there?"

I took a deep breath. "Yes. Sorry. Hi Uncle Bill."

"Your aunt and I had a long talk about this Malcolm situation. Needless to say, I'm not at all happy about it. On the one hand, I understand that you still have feelings for him, and that makes it very difficult for you to see this objectively. I understand that. And I know you want to be fair. You've always tried to be fair to everyone. That's probably what got you into this mess in the first place." As his voice got louder. I heard Aunt Vickie say something. He continued in a calmer tone. "As I said, I'm not happy about this situation at all. However, I've agreed with your aunt that we'll give it a try. I would rather we know what's going on than you see him behind our backs. So, thanks for telling us. Just know this: if he hurts a hair on your head, he will be sorry." His voice rose again.

"Thank you, Uncle Bill. I promise you; you won't regret it. I do feel strongly that I should support him. He really is trying to be a better person."

"Well, bring him to brunch on Sunday and we'll meet him, and I'll decide for myself. Let me pass you back to your aunt."

I chatted with Aunt Vickie for a few minutes. As soon as I hung up, I peeped out the window. Still no sign of Malcolm's camper. I decided to get an early night and talk to him the next day.

CHAPTER SEVENTEEN

As I left for work the following morning, Malcolm's camper was back in the driveway. I was in a hurry so didn't stop to talk with him, anyway he was probably still asleep. We were having dinner together later; I'd tell him then.

It was a busy day, and I didn't have time to think about anything but work. Finally, as security locked the doors, I packed up and slipped out before anyone delayed me. When I got home, Malcolm was sitting on the doorstep waiting. He stood up as I walked up the path and stepped to one side so that I could open the door.

"You should give me a key. That way, I can take the dog out for a walk while you are at work."

I didn't answer. Not only did I not want to give him a key. I also didn't want him taking Hawn out. At least, not without me. Her training was progressing nicely, and I didn't want anyone else messing that up.

"Sally? Did you hear me?"

"Yes, sorry. The trainer I go to said that only one person should work with her until her training is at a certain stage. He said she would just get confused. Sorry." I took a deep breath and stepped back, watching him.

"You don't have to be afraid of me. I told you, anger management, remember? It works. Unlike Hawn, I have completed my training. I promise you, I won't hurt you ever again."

I nodded and tried to smile. It was going to be hard to believe; hard to trust.

"Let's go take her for a walk and then we can have dinner," I said.

After thirty minutes of going through Hawn's exercises, I let her loose in the dog park to play. Malcolm and I sat on a bench watching her and chatting. I told him about my lunch with Aunt Vickie. That Uncle Bill was prepared to give him a chance, and that they had invited him to brunch on Sunday. He told me about his fruitless job search.

"You know, Sal, I think I should try the rideshare option."

"In your camper?"

"No, of course not. I could use your car. You don't use it during the day anyway, in fact some days you don't use it at all. I would put gas in it, of course, and pay for any servicing." He paused, looking at me, clearly waiting for a reply. "What do you think?" he added when I said nothing.

I didn't know what to say. I could see that he was trying to worm his way back into my life. It was too fast, and while I wanted him there, I was still very nervous about trusting him again.

"I suppose so," I said. "Yes, that seems like a good idea until you can find something permanent," I added, in case he thought I didn't want to help him. Of course, I wanted to help him. It was just that I didn't want to let him take control of my life again.

As soon as I called Hawn, she responded immediately. She was such an intelligent dog; she was learning fast.

When we got back to the apartment, after I fed and watered Hawn, I set about preparing dinner. Malcolm surprised me by offering to help. I was going to say no, but stopped myself. If he'd changed, then I should, too. I asked him to set the table.

After dinner, he helped me to clear the table and stack the dishwasher. I couldn't ever remember him doing that before. Maybe this would work.

"Oh, here," I said, handing him the spare keys to my car. "The only thing is, if it's raining, I'll need to drive to work, or you can drive me?"

"Sure, I can drive you to work if the weather's bad, or if you just don't feel like walking. That'll work. Thanks."

We stood in the kitchen in awkward silence for a few minutes.

"I guess I'd better let you go to bed. You've got work tomorrow." Malcolm said, turning towards the door. He paused and turned back. Looking at me, he said, "Would it be okay to kiss you goodnight?"

I moved towards him, and he put his arms around me, kissing me gently, then with more fervor. We stepped apart, breathless.

"Goodnight Sal. Sleep well. See you tomorrow." He turned around and hurried out, closing the door behind him.

I locked up, said goodnight to Hawn and went to bed, wishing that my life was not so complicated.

~~

The following morning, the weather was dry. I was happy to walk to work. I was not sure how I would feel about Malcolm driving me. It might feel too much like back in Austin when we drove to work together.

When I got home that evening, the car was gone. After Hawn's walk, Malcolm was once again waiting on the doorstep, this time with a six-pack of beer. It was Friday evening. I was glad that he said nothing about giving him a key. He didn't ask permission to kiss me, either. He just went ahead and kissed me lightly on the lips before asking me how my day was. Like it was a perfectly normal thing to do. Nothing was normal about this. I wondered if it would ever be. When I'd prepared dinner, we sat down with a beer.

"My news," Malcolm said with a grin. "I start rideshare on Monday."

"That's great news. At least that should placate Uncle Bill on Sunday."

"Why? Does he need placating?" Malcolm frowned.

"Well, naturally, he's feeling a bit worried. I mean, he knows our history together, and he's very protective."

Malcolm got himself another beer and sat down again before saying, "Tell me about them, your uncle and aunt."

"Uncle Bill was my dad's brother. He's a professor at Harvard. Aunt Vickie writes poetry. I came to live with them when I was fifteen, after my parents died. I told you all that when we first met." As soon as the words were out, I held my breath, hoping he didn't get annoyed.

"Yeah, but I wasn't likely to meet them then, so it didn't matter much to me. I didn't even remember you had relatives living here, not until I saw that bank newsletter. So, what were you doing in Austin?"

"I grew up there. When I graduated from Harvard, I wanted to go back."

He studied me for a few minutes as he finished off his beer. "And now you are back here again—because of me."

I took a drink of my beer and said nothing. I wasn't sure what to say, and I didn't want to say anything to upset him. Would I ever come to fully trust him again? I wondered. In one way, that felt right. Why would you trust someone who had hurt you so badly? On the other hand, if he's working so hard to be a better person, why wouldn't I support him? I was so confused.

"But your uncle's prepared to meet me on Sunday, so I guess that's a good thing? Right?"

"Oh, yes, it is. Both Aunt Vickie and Uncle Bill are prepared to give you a second chance. For my sake." I smiled at him, watching for any sign of anger. He looked down at his empty beer bottle for a few seconds, saying nothing.

"Let's have another beer and eat." He said, going to the fridge.

Over dinner, we agreed he would come with me to Hawn's training session the following day. He wanted to watch and learn so that he could help. Then, in the afternoon, we'd take a drive so he could get familiar with the area. He was going to have to rely on GPS for most of his driving, but it would help.

Before he left, he put his arms around me and hugged me tight.

"I'm so very sorry for what I did to you, Sal. I hope you'll be able to trust me again." He whispered.

There was a lump in my throat, and I couldn't answer him. That was just as well, because I didn't want to tell him I didn't know if I ever would. As he kissed me goodnight, I felt that fluttering in my stomach that he used to cause when we first met. *Perhaps that was a good sign?* I thought as I locked the door behind him.

~~

To say I was nervous on Sunday morning was an understatement. It didn't help that Malcolm asked if he could take a shower. Seeing him come out of the bathroom with just a small towel wrapped around him almost caused my heart to stop. Though I have to say I did question the small towel. There were large bath towels hanging in the bathroom and I'd even put out a bathrobe for him. I suspected he used the smallest towel deliberately. He knew he had a great body. He was just reminding me of that fact.

"Sorry babe, could I borrow some deodorant?"

"Sure, it's in the bathroom cabinet."

He went back and closed the door. Twenty minutes later, he came out again, this time fully dressed. He still looked good.

We arrived a few minutes early, and as we turned into the driveway. Malcolm stood still and stared at the house.

"Gee. That's a mansion!" he said. "Three stories and look at those turrets! Professors must get paid well."

"I guess. Aunt Vickie's poetry sells well, too, I think."

"Poetry? Who would buy that?"

I shrugged, not wanting to get into a conversation that just might annoy him. He was always very touchy about the fact that he didn't have a degree.

"Come on, let's go in." I led the way around the side of the house to the backyard. As it came into sight, I heard Malcolm gasp. It was a big yard, lined with old trees and flowerbeds. The patio was also big, with a covered area and an outdoor kitchen.

Uncle Bill and Aunt Vickie were sitting under an umbrella. When Hawn saw them, she started wagging her tail furiously and looking at me. I undid her leash, and she rushed over to them. They both stood up and came to greet us.

While Aunt Vickie hugged me, Uncle Bill shook hands with Malcolm. Then Aunt Vickie hugged Malcolm. That did surprise me. I was very grateful to them for making such an effort to accept him and give him another chance to prove he could be trusted. I knew it was not easy for them.

"I wanted to bring you flowers, but I don't start work until tomorrow. But looking at your wonderful yard, I see you already have more than I could possibly bring you," Malcolm said to Aunt Vickie.

"Oh goodness, that's not necessary," she said. "Come and sit down and have a drink." She poured mimosas and handed them out as we sat down.

Malcolm dialed up the charm. He was always good at that. Uncle Bill said very little, but I noticed him watching Malcolm. Aunt Vickie seemed to be falling under his spell. I was not sure if that was a good thing or not. I know I was very glad when it was time to leave. But it was a relief to have that meeting over with. I would have to wait to get the verdict from Aunt Vickie. I made a mental note to arrange a lunch with her the following week.

CHAPTER EIGHTEEN

The weather on Monday morning was cooler but still good for walking. As I left the house, Malcolm climbed out of his camper.

"Just checking to see if you needed a ride to work?"

"No. Thanks. I prefer to walk whenever possible. You take the car, and good luck today."

"Thanks. Have a good day yourself."

I hurried towards work, hoping that he managed to pick up a few rides on his first day. We hadn't talked about money, but I imagined he was running low. I knew that when he left Austin, he'd cashed in his 401K and had some savings. So hopefully he had enough to last to his first paycheck. Luckily, the car was a hybrid, so it was not too expensive on gas.

It was a busy morning, but I got a chance to text Aunt Vickie and arrange lunch later in the week. During the afternoon, the skies were dark with storm clouds. I looked out the window and hoped that it would hold off until I got home. I was out of luck. By four, the rain hammered on the windows. At four forty-five, I got a text.

Malcolm: I'm parked outside the bank.

Me: Brilliant! I'll be out shortly. Thank you.

I stuck my head around the door of Mark's office to let him know I had a ride home, so was heading out a few minutes early. Then packed up and left. The rain drenched me in just the few feet between the bank and the car. I jumped in and slammed the door.

"Phew, thanks so much for picking me up."

Malcolm just smiled and squeezed my hand as he started up the engine.

"I'll have to take Hawn to the indoor dog park today. Thank goodness I bought that membership."

"That's a cool idea. An indoor park."

"It is. I joined so we would have somewhere to go through the winter. I still prefer being outside, of course. How was your day?"

"I've been working flat out all day. It looks very promising, though I suppose the weather helped."

It surprised me to see so few dogs in the park. Probably because of the thunder. Thunder terrifies most dogs. Not Hawn, she growls back at it, but it doesn't seem to bother her too much. Just the same, we didn't stay too long.

By the time we got home, the trees were creaking and bending. Malcolm's camper was literally rocking back and forth. We made a dash for the front door and slammed it shut against the wind.

"You can't sleep in that camper tonight. It isn't safe. If the wind gets any worse, it could turn it over."

Malcolm said nothing, but the way he looked at me was unsettling. Before he got any ideas, I added, "I'll make up the couch for you. It folds out into a bed."

"Thanks. I appreciate that." I couldn't help thinking he looked a little disappointed.

Next morning, I went into the kitchen to make coffee, but Malcolm was already up, and coffee was ready.

"Thanks." I said, pouring myself a cup. "This is a pleasant surprise."

"The rain's still coming down. I'll drive you to work as soon as you're ready. I've already taken Hawn out to potty."

"Oh, thanks for that." I could get used to this new side of Malcolm, and it was nice to have someone else to help.

By the end of the day, the wind had died down, but it was still raining. Malcolm once again was waiting outside the bank when I came out. Unfortunately, Amanda was right behind me and watched with interest as I climbed into the passenger seat. I knew I was in for an interrogation the following day. Oh well, it was bound to happen sooner or later.

Malcolm had another busy day and received quite a few cash tips, so he had bought a bottle of sparkling wine to celebrate. He poured us both a glass as I was preparing dinner.

"I have some bad news as well." He said, continuing before I had time to get upset. "The camper flooded last night. I checked on it before I came to collect you and it looks like there is a leak in the sunroof. Is it okay if I sleep here till I get it sorted?"

"Yes, of course. That's such a bummer."

"Thanks, babe." He came around the counter and hugged me. "Here, let me top up your glass."

~~

I was right. Next morning Amanda came into the kitchen as I was making the coffee. It was early for her to be in the office. I found it hard to believe that she came in early just to question me. But that is exactly what she did.

"Good morning, Sally! I see you've got a new boyfriend. This one's definitely better looking than Sam." She laughed.

"No, he's actually an old friend from Austin," I said, hoping she would leave it at that. No such luck.

"Oh. Is he staying with you? Just came to visit, did he?"

"Yes, he's staying with me, and he has moved here." I filled my mug and left before she had a chance to ask any more questions. No doubt the news delighted her. She didn't have competition for Mark's attention. I almost felt sorry for her.

As I sat down at my desk, my phone pinged. A text from Aunt Vickie confirming lunch for today. I hadn't forgotten. I'd mixed feelings about it. Of course, I love to spend time with Aunt Vickie, and I wanted to get their reactions to Malcolm. On the other hand, I was worried those reactions would not be positive.

Aunt Vickie was sitting looking over the menu when I arrived at the restaurant. I hugged her and sat down.

"What a storm that was," she said. "Okay, that's enough small talk. Let's discuss Malcolm."

That was so like her. No wasting time, straight to the point. It was just one of the things I loved about her.

"So, what did you think? And what did Uncle Bill think?"

"I'm amazed to say, despite what we know he did to you. We liked him. If we hadn't known about how he hurt you, seen the injuries for ourselves, we would never question you getting involved with him." She paused and looked at me over her glasses. "I just hope that the anger management thing cured him—or whatever the correct terminology is."

"I know. Obviously, I have reservations. It's hard to trust him again. But he really seems to have completely changed."

"Your uncle said something interesting. He said if he had been an alcoholic and attended Alcoholics Anonymous, would we give him another chance?"

"Gosh. I never looked at it that way. That's so true. With an alcoholic, you know there's always a chance they'll drink again. But you have to give them support." I have to say, putting it that way, it made a lot of sense to me. The comparison somehow made me feel much better.

As we left the restaurant, Aunt Vickie told me that Malcolm would be welcome any time.

"See you both on Sunday, for brunch? And Hawn too, of course."

I hugged her and told her we would be there. I hurried back to work, hoping that I could avoid Amanda for the afternoon. That would not happen.

"Lunch with the new man?" Amanda said way too loudly, as I passed her on my way to my office. Everyone looked up. "What's his name, anyway?"

"His name's Malcolm, and he's not a new man. He is an old friend." I sighed, adding, "And no, I didn't have lunch with him."

As I sat down at my desk, Betty came in.

"What was Amanda going on about now?"

"Oh. An old friend from Austin is in town. She saw him pick me up outside when it was raining. Naturally, she is all over it."

Betty left my office chuckling to herself.

That evening, it surprised me to see Malcolm parked outside the bank again.

"You don't need to come pick me up if the weather's good. I like walking," I said, getting into the car.

"I know, sorry. But I never got a key from you, so I thought it was easier to wait here rather than outside the apartment."

"Oh. Sorry about that. I'll give you one when we get home." I didn't feel so bad about giving him a key since talking with Aunt Vickie.

After dinner, we sat on the couch watching an old movie, *Ghost*. I don't know exactly how it happened; I guess it was the movie, but suddenly Malcolm wrapped his arms around me, and we were kissing. That familiar fluttering in my stomach rose to my chest and suddenly the tension left my body and I relaxed into him. The movie faded into the background. It was like a first kiss. I can't explain it; time seemed to stand still. I don't even remember how it happened; we were both naked in my bed. We'd made love before. We'd had sex before. But nothing like that. I could tell Malcolm felt the same. He was staring into my eyes, gently stroking my cheek. I'd never seen such a tender look on his face. I dared to believe we could make this work after all.

"Thank you for trusting me. I love you," Malcolm said, as he kissed me. A long, gentle kiss. "Goodnight."

"Goodnight. I love you too."

CHAPTER NINETEEN

Over dinner a few weeks later, Malcolm told me he was thinking of getting the camper completely overhauled. After the damage from the storm, it was no longer usable, but he believed it could be brought back to life.

"It would be a way we could go off for weekends without costing too much. Visit some of the National Parks and stay in the camper. What do you think?"

I was still not used to him asking my opinion. Ever since the night he ended up in my bed, he had stayed in it; well, at night anyway. He officially moved in. He was working continuously doing rideshare and making good money. He was paying part of the rent and other expenses and could easily afford to have the camper renovated. I thought it was a great idea. Besides, it was an eyesore as it was. I was afraid one of the neighbors would complain to the landlord.

"We might even be able to keep it at Uncle Bill's place when we're not using it," I said.

Uncle Bill and Aunt Vickie had really warmed to Malcolm. Everything was going so well. Then we bumped into Amanda.

I continued to walk to and from work, except if it was raining. Then Malcolm dropped me off in the morning and picked me up in the evening. Occasionally, he would wait outside the bank on a fine evening. Because he was passing, he said. It didn't happen very often, so I let it go.

The evening he met Amanda, it was not raining. Betty and I were standing outside the bank chatting when he pulled up and got out of the car. He came over to us and introduced himself to Betty. Just at that moment, Amanda came out. Naturally, she couldn't resist joining us and introducing herself. Then she made some remark about him frightening off my stalker.

"What stalker? Someone has been stalking you?" Malcolm's voice was harsh, a tone I used to hear quite often, but not since he came to Cambridge. I drew a deep breath, but before I could say anything, Amanda started telling him about the times Sam had been hanging around the bank and the camera with the zoom lens. I caught him looking at me with a strange expression on his face. He said nothing more, and we said goodbye and climbed into the car.

"You never mentioned you had a stalker." He said, keeping his eyes on the road.

"It never occurred to me to mention it. To be honest, I'd forgotten about him. But Amanda's right. You will definitely have frightened him off. Thank you for that, too." I hoped that my voice sounded light and unconcerned.

He glanced at me briefly. "You're welcome. Who the hell is he?"

"Oh, just some guy I made the mistake of going out to dinner with once or twice. I think he has a screw loose. I reported him to the police and I haven't seen him since. That was ages ago now."

We drove the rest of the way in silence. That night, we had sex. Malcolm didn't make love to me. He had sex with me. There was none of the tenderness he had surprised me with. In its place was an undertone of anger and an overtone of control. He didn't say a word and had never been so rough when we'd had sex before. I felt like I was being raped. It was as though the new Malcolm had disappeared to be replaced by the old one, the abuser I had managed to escape and was fool enough to let back in.

When he finished, he apologized.

"Oh, God Sal. I'm so sorry. I shouldn't have done that. I was jealous."

I tried, but I couldn't stop the tears.

"You've nothing to be jealous of. Sam, the guy who was stalking me. He was horrible. The reason I stopped seeing him was because he was stalking his previous girlfriend. He was nothing to me. Except a nuisance and an embarrassment."

But the damage was done. I saw a slight flash of the old Malcolm and all the doubts came rushing back. I was once again on edge and watching him and everything I said to him.

~~

For the next few days, I felt like I was walking on ice. Terrified I would slip and upset Malcolm. I realized that was no way to live, but I wasn't sure how to fix it, other than tiptoe around him.

Then on Thursday evening, I got a call from Ted.

"Hi Sally. I wonder if we could ask for your help with a victim again?"

"Sure Ted, what do you need me to do?"

"Well, our victim, Barbara, needs to be picked up in New Haven and transported to Salem. We know you're working full time, so she'll stay in New Haven until Saturday. If you could do it then, that would be great?"

"Saturday would be no problem. I can do that."

"Great, thanks. Let me give you the details."

I could see Malcolm looking at me with a black look on his face.

"What the hell was that?" he said when I hung up.

I didn't quite know what to say. We hadn't spoken about Caitlin and her Escape Route, though I knew he knew about it. After all, he had gone to jail for breaking into her home after she helped me to get away.

"That was Ted. He works with Caitlin and—" I took a step back as Malcolm jumped to his feet and stood in front of me, both fists balled and his mouth in a snarl.

"Caitlin! That bitch! She's the reason I spent six months in prison! What did they want?"

"They want me to give someone a ride to Salem on Saturday. I'll need the car." I was determined that he would not stop me from doing the one thing I felt I had to do.

He stood there for a few seconds, saying nothing. I was terrified he was going to hit me. Hawn got up from her bed and came over and stood beside me. She didn't make a sound, but she was staring at Malcolm. He turned around and stomped out of the apartment.

Next morning, he was all smiles and apologies.

"Sorry Sal. I need to control myself better than that. I'll do better. I promise." He said as he drove me to work. In the evening, he picked me up from work and insisted that we go out to eat. I really didn't want to, as I had an early start in the morning, but I agreed to avoid upsetting him.

When I woke up on Saturday morning, it surprised me to discover Malcolm was already up. I guessed he was making breakfast, still trying to make amends. He wasn't. I panicked and rushed to open the front door. The car was gone. I tried calling him, but he didn't pick up. Finally, I called Aunt Vickie to see if I could borrow her car for the day.

"Sorry for the short notice. Malcolm must have forgotten that I needed the car, and he took it."

"Certainly dear, I've nothing planned for today and it's in a very good cause. Let me drive over there now and you can drop me back."

"Thank you so much. Would you mind if I left Hawn with you today? I'm not sure when Malcolm will be back."

"Not at all. We love having her."

Twenty minutes later, I dropped Aunt Vickie and Hawn at her place and was on the road. A little late but I could still keep to schedule. Luckily, because of the long distance, I was confident I could make up the time.

~~

It took me about two and a half hours to get to New Haven and find the address.

"Hi. I'm Sally," I said as a young woman answered my knock. "I'm here to pick up Barbara."

Barbara, my passenger, was older than me. In her mid-forties, I guessed. She looked worn out. She seemed to be in a hurry. Luckily, I didn't want to wait around either. The sooner I got home, the less likely Malcolm would be there. I expected him to stay away the entire day, to avoid any chance of me taking the car.

"It should take less than three hours to get to Salem," I said to her as we drove off. "If you want to snooze, go ahead. If you want to talk, I'm happy to listen. I was once a victim too, so I know what you are feeling right now."

"Thank you, Sally. I appreciate all that you're doing for me." She rested her head against the window and closed her eyes.

I assumed that meant she didn't want to talk. We drove in silence for about an hour. Suddenly, Barbara woke up and let out a yelp.

"Are you alright?" I asked her. "Do you need me to stop?"

"No. No, thanks. It was just a bad dream."

"Oh, okay. Don't worry, they'll subside in time."

"You think so?" She sounded dubious.

"I'm sure of it. Therapy has a tendency to make it worse at first, but once you face it and learn the lesson, they'll fade away."

"I hope so." She said, dabbing at her eyes with a tissue. "I'm a widow. My husband was a wonderful man. We were very happy. He died two years ago."

I just nodded, wondering what she was doing in the Escape Route. Then she continued.

"Last year, I decided to try to find another man. I hoped to find someone as good, to share my life with and be happy again."

"What happened?"

"I signed up for a dating app and started meeting men. A lot of much younger men tried to date me. Turns out they think older women are desperate for sex. Then I met Frank." She went silent for a few miles.

I waited. Remembering what it was like to be in her place right then. She sighed and continued.

"He was wonderful, at first. Then, after I moved in with him, he suddenly became controlling and bullying. It wasn't long before he got violent. The first time I thought it was because he was drunk, and I had antagonized him." She looked at me. "Never excuse abuse, no matter what the reason. There is no excuse for it."

"I did learn that. At least—I hope I learned it."

"If you didn't, take my word for it now. It's inexcusable. Walk away. Run away. The second time was worse, and I did run away."

"Good for you."

"And now I know it's impossible to recreate the past. What I had before is gone. I can't do anything about it." She dabbed her eyes again and sighed.

We continued the rest of the drive in silence.

When I dropped her off in Salem, before she got out of the car, she turned to me.

"Thank you, Sally. Take care of yourself and remember what I said."

I drove back to Aunt Vickie's thinking about her words. Hoping that I didn't have to run away again.

I dropped the car off. Aunt Vickie wanted me to stay, but I said I had things to do at home.

"Well, let me drive you back."

"No thanks. I need to walk after all that driving." I headed home with Hawn.

Luckily, Malcolm was still gone. By the time he got home, I'd cleaned up and made dinner. He never mentioned a word about taking the car and I decided it was best to just say nothing. I needed to figure out a way to correct the series of mistakes I'd made, and was still making, before I said anything to him that might let him know what I was thinking.

CHAPTER TWENTY

After that, things between me and Malcolm were once again strained. Of course, now that he was living with me, it was much more difficult. He seemed to sense that I no longer trusted him. He made huge efforts to convince me that everything was fine. But it wasn't. I finally realized that no matter how hard he tried to change, the old Malcolm was still in there somewhere. It frightened me. I also felt incredibly stupid for ever believing it could be otherwise. I was determined that this time I would not run away, as Barbara had advised. Apart from the fact that I had nowhere to run to. I needed to stop the cycle once and for all.

On Friday morning, Malcolm offered to drive me to work. I refused. The weather was beautiful, and I wanted to walk.

"Oh, by the way, I'll be a little late this evening. One of the tellers is heading off on maternity leave and we're doing a send-off for her. You know? The usual stuff," I said as I was leaving.

"How late? Do you want me to take Hawn for a walk?"

"Oh no, not that late. Just about thirty minutes. See you this evening."

He walked me to the door, and before opening it, he kissed me.

"How about we go out to dinner this evening? After Hawn's walk?" he said.

"Sure, that would be nice."

~~

After security locked the doors that evening, we all gathered in the kitchen. Mark presented Jo with a gift, flowers, and a card signed by everyone. Then we had a glass of sparkling, non-alcoholic wine. Twenty minutes after closing time, we all poured out of the bank together.

"Can I give you a ride home?" Mark asked me.

"No, thanks. I like to walk when the weather's good. See you Monday." As I turned to leave, I spotted Malcolm pull up. "Looks like I won't be walking after all," I said, as I headed towards him, turning to give Mark a quick wave. He waved back and headed across the road.

"Who was that guy?" Malcolm asked, staring after him.

"Who? Oh, Mark? He's my boss, the Bank Manager."

"What were you talking about?"

"Nothing, he just offered me a ride home."

"Does he often give you a ride home?"

"No! Of course not. You know that I either walk or you come and get me. In fact, that's the first time we've left at the same time."

"Okay, let's get Hawn her walk and we can head out for a nice dinner," Malcolm said in a more cheerful tone, as he glanced across the road towards the parking lot again, before pulling out.

Dinner was nice. We went to a fancy restaurant and had a fabulous meal. Malcolm maintained a cheerful conversation. As we were leaving, he thanked our server and left a large tip. None of this was the behavior he'd shown back in Austin. Even when I first met him. Still, I didn't feel comfortable.

"Now, I've a surprise for you," he announced as we walked to the car.

"Really? What?"

"Wouldn't be a surprise if I told you, now, would it?"

We drove in silence for about twenty minutes, then he pulled into Uncle Bill's driveway. There was the camper. At least, I assumed it was the same camper. It looked completely different, almost new.

"Wow! What a transformation," I said, hurrying to get out of the car.

Uncle Bill and Aunt Vickie came out of the house and joined us. Malcolm proudly showed us the inside. A tiny kitchen and comfortable bench seat both looked brand new. With the flick of a switch, the top raised up to reveal a bed with a small ladder under the tent-like roofing.

"Not a lot of space, but enough for two people to cook, eat and sleep. What do you think?" Malcolm was watching me as I stared around.

"It's amazing! Such an improvement."

He smiled happily. "Yes, and they replaced the engine too, so it's as reliable as a new vehicle."

"I am so impressed!" Uncle Bill said. "This is the way to camp!"

Aunt Vickie laughed dubiously. "I don't know. I think I still prefer the comfort of a good hotel. But I guess it is most definitely more economical," she said.

"Thanks for letting us keep it here, Bill," Malcolm said.

"No problem at all. We have the space so it's not in the way."

We told them we would take the camper out in the morning, said goodbye, and headed home.

~~

The following day, we walked with Hawn to pick up the camper. Our plan was to spend the day at a National Park about twenty miles away, as a trial run.

About forty minutes later, we parked and got out to look around. We selected one of the hiking trails and set off. Hawn was very excited with all the fresh scents and sounds; she behaved remarkably well, considering it was such an unfamiliar experience for her.

The trail took us in a loop. Two hours later, we arrived back at the camper. I was grateful that I did so much walking. Between exercising Hawn, every day since I got her and walking to and from work, I was pretty fit. But I was tired and ready to sit down and relax. Malcolm was exhausted. He occasionally came walking with me and Hawn, but the rest of the time he was sitting in a car driving around. He stretched out on one of the camp chairs and groaned. I got a bowl of water for Hawn and a bottle of water for myself, and one for Malcolm, before joining him.

"This is so beautiful," I said, looking off across the patch of green into the forest.

Malcolm opened his eyes and looked around. "Yeah, I guess it is nice." Then he closed his eyes again. Hawn stretched out at my feet and went to sleep.

After about thirty minutes, I got bored. Malcolm and Hawn were both fast asleep. I climbed into the camper to fix something to eat. I had brought some pre-prepared meals. They just needed to go in the oven for 40 minutes. The tiny kitchen had a small, fitted oven. I also brought a bottle of wine. I put the meals in the oven, poured myself a glass of wine, and went back outside. As I sat down again, Malcolm woke up.

"I have just put the food on. We can eat in about an hour. Would you like a glass of wine?"

"Yeah. That sounds good."

"You wouldn't have this much fun with your friend Mark." He said as he took the glass of wine I offered him.

"What? Mark? He's my boss, not my friend. I'm not sure what you mean?"

"I saw the way he looked at you. He definitely wants to be more than just your friend."

"Where did that come from? Have you been stewing on this since yesterday?"

"First, I hear you have a stalker, then I see that boss of yours eying you up. I can't decide if you're just a flirt or if you're a whore," he said, emptying the glass and handing it to me with a wide grin. "Just joking Sal, lighten up."

I tried to smile and pretend I found it funny. Remembering that when he got into this sort of mood before, it was best to stay quiet.

Taking the glass, I put it on the counter in the kitchen and checked on the food.

"Won't be long now and we can eat," I said, sitting down again.

"How about some more wine?"

"Oh, I thought it would be nice to save the second glass to go with the food. Is that okay with you?"

"Okay, I guess." He got up, groaned, and stretched. Then wandered off towards the public restrooms on the other side of the parking area.

After we'd eaten, we packed everything back in the camper and headed home. One thing was for sure: Hawn wouldn't need a walk when we got back. We parked the camper at the apartment that night. We were all ready to just sit down for the rest of the evening and do nothing.

"We can drive over in the camper in the morning, and park it at Bill's then," Malcolm said.

For the rest of the weekend, except while we were having brunch with Uncle Bill and Aunt Vickie, Malcolm kept referring to Sam and

Mark. Although he tried to disguise his comments as jokes, I could see that he was jealous. I could also see more signs of the old Malcolm. He was doing what he used to do. Building up a head of steam and I feared it would eventually blow. I swore to myself that if he lifted a finger towards me, I would tell him to leave. I realized I should have been more aware. He was already being abusive; I should have told him to go as soon as he started being controlling.

I was blind and now it's getting out of hand.

CHAPTER TWENTY-ONE

I was glad when Monday morning finally came around. As I was leaving for work, he mentioned he planned to come into the bank to open an account. He suggested we have lunch together.

"Sure, good idea. I can take lunch around twelve-thirty, if that works for you?"

All morning, I was on edge. I could understand that he needed to open a bank account, but why my bank? That would be so awkward. Every time a customer came in, I looked up to see if it was him. Finally, at about midday, he came in and, as luck would have it, Amanda was free and led him into one of the empty offices. Our offices were like glass boxes, built along the one wall in the bank that had windows. This allowed the light to come through into the building. It also meant that he could see through to my office. Only Mark's office was on the opposite side, beside the tellers. It was more private, with walls instead of glass.

At twelve-fifteen, Mark came and walked across the foyer. I watched out of the corner of my eye, hoping he was not going to my office. He was. It would have been comical if it were not such a problem. Both Amanda and Malcolm turned around and watched him walk across the floor of the bank. He sat down opposite me. They both continued to watch. I wondered if they had completed the work of opening his account, or just abandoned it to stare at us.

Our business completed, Mark stood up and headed back to his own office. Again, their heads turned to follow him back. When his door closed, they turned to each other and continued as though nothing had happened. I got up and went to the restroom. By the time I came out a few minutes later, Malcolm was waiting for me. He hugged me in the middle of the bank, much to my embarrassment. However, I wasn't sure why I should feel embarrassed. I think it was because I doubted his motives were pure.

Lunch was very uncomfortable. Malcolm wanted to know what Mark was talking to me about. I told him it was bank business, and I couldn't speak about it. That annoyed him, but he knew I was right. He also knew that I wouldn't break that rule. Then he told me that Amanda had mentioned that Mark was interested in me.

"That's ridiculous Malcolm. The problem is that Amanda is interested in Mark and she's jealous of anyone he speaks to. Plus, she expected to get the AM job. It pissed her off when she didn't get it."

He wouldn't let it go. It was a relief when it was time to go back to the office.

That evening, once again, he was waiting outside the bank for me.

"You really don't have to pick me up unless it's raining. I actually enjoy walking home. It helps me to decompress after work." I said, as I got in.

"Oh, and then you can get a ride home from Mark, I suppose?"

"No. Of course not, I enjoy the walk. I enjoy the solitude to just think and relax."

"So now I am preventing you from relaxing?" He glared at me.

"That's not what I said." I knew it was time to just shut up and hope that he calmed down.

He didn't.

~~

For almost the entire time we walked Hawn, Malcolm sulked. He sat watching me put her through her training routine, with a dark look on his face. Dinner was the same. He sat surfing through the channels on the TV while I prepared the meal. He didn't offer to help and didn't set the table. I could see he was back to his old self. Perhaps anger management only worked if you keep attending.

After dinner, I cleared the table and joined him on the couch.

"What's up Malcolm? We were doing so well up to recently."

"We were doing fine until you started back to your old ways. Flirting and shit."

"I keep telling you, I've no interest in Mark. He's a nice guy and a great boss, but I'm not interested in him romantically. I'm not flirting with him or anyone else."

"What about your stalker? You dated him!"

"You and I were not together then. And I stopped dating him before you turned up. Do you think I enjoy being stalked? It's a horrible feeling. I hated it and I hated having to go to the police. And tell Uncle Bill. Most of all, I hated telling Mark." As soon as the words were out, I knew it was a mistake.

"What did you need to tell Mark for? You were looking for attention from him? Sympathy?"

"No. No. The police said I needed to tell my employer."

Suddenly, he jumped to his feet and threw a cushion at me. Shouting obscenities.

After that, all hell broke loose.

Hawn jumped to her feet and lunged at him, growling. Before she reached him, he lashed out and kicked her. She yelped as she slammed against the wall. She tried to stand up, then howled and collapsed.

Malcolm went over to her and bent down. I rushed over and shoved him aside.

"Don't you dare touch her."

He lost his balance and fell over. I grabbed my bag and gathered her up in my arms and staggered out to the car. As I loaded her into the back seat, he came running out and attempted to climb into the driver's seat.

"Get away, get away from us." I tried to push him aside.

"I'm sorry Sally. I was just protecting myself. I didn't mean to hurt her. Let me drive you to the vet's office." He grabbed my hand and tried to pull me away from the car door.

"Don't you lay a hand on me. Get away." He stepped back, a surprised look on his face. I jumped into the car and slammed the door and drove off.

I knew that my local vet had evening hours for emergencies. They were about to close when I arrived. The vet did a full examination and an x-ray. I waited impatiently until he finally came and told me she had a fractured leg, and he would need to pin it. I told him to please do whatever he needed to fix her.

Two hours later, he led me into his kennel area to see her. She was groggy but happy to see me. A series of metal screws kept a bar in place to stabilize the damaged bone. It looked awful.

"She'll be fine. It was a clean break. She's strong and healthy and will heal fast. But we'll keep her here overnight for observation," he said.

"Thank you so much. How much do I owe you?"

"It'll be approximately fifteen hundred. I can give you an exact figure tomorrow when you pick her up."

As I drove home, I couldn't stop crying. At one point, I had to pull over because I couldn't see properly. Sitting in the car, on the side of the road, I cried until I just ran out of tears.

When I eventually got home, it was late, but Malcolm was still up. He opened the door as soon as I pulled into the driveway.

"How is she? Where is she?" he said, opening the back door and looking at the empty back seat.

"She's still at the vet. She had to have an operation to fix her leg. You broke it. The vet's keeping her overnight."

"Oh my God, Sally. I'm so sorry. It was a reflex reaction. I never meant to hurt her. I'll pay the vet, whatever it costs. I'll pay it." He tried to put his arms around me, and I pushed him away.

"Leave me alone Malcolm. Just leave me alone. I should ask you to leave. And I will if you ever lift a finger to me, or Hawn, again. For now, you can go back to sleeping on the couch."

I probably should have kicked him out then. Hindsight's a wonderful thing.

CHAPTER TWENTY-TWO

I called the vet first thing the next morning. Hawn was doing well and ready to be collected. Next, I called Mark and let him know I needed to take the day off.

"I hope you're alright? Anything I can do to help?" he said.

"No, thanks. I'm fine. My dog had an accident last night and I need to pick her up from the vet this morning. I would prefer to stay with her for the day to make sure she's okay. I'll be in tomorrow."

Then I told Malcolm that I was taking the car to get Hawn and he could have it when I got back. He said nothing, just nodded.

When I got back with Hawn, Malcolm came out and wanted to help me carry her in. Although she was getting quite big, I refused to let him help. I didn't want him touching her. Hawn had already appeared to have forgotten that he'd hurt her.

As soon as I put her down, she struggled to stand up and started limping around the room, then she flopped down at my feet and fell asleep. The vet had given me a waterproof cover for her leg. He said to put it on when taking her outside, and that I could start doing so immediately. Short walks at first, he assured me he had fully stabilized the leg, and it shouldn't give her any problems.

I spent the day catching up on household chores I'd been putting off. In the afternoon, I took Hawn out for a short walk. She was very excited and hobbled along willingly.

The following morning, Malcolm offered to drive me to work, but I refused.

"The weather's fine and I would prefer to walk." I said, closing the door firmly behind me.

As I walked, I tried to figure out the mess I had once again gotten myself into. I finally accepted that I had no future with Malcolm. I also knew that I should have told him to leave when he kicked Hawn. But while he could live comfortably in his camper, and he had done it before, my car was his only means of income. If I kicked him out, he would have no way to support himself. But why should I feel responsible for that? I shouldn't. I knew that. But I did.

When I got into the bank, everyone wanted to know how Hawn was and what had happened to her. A part of me wanted to say, "Malcolm kicked her, and I kicked him out." I knew that was what I should have been able to say. What the hell was wrong with me? I guess I shouldn't have stopped seeing the therapist. Maybe I needed to go back.

During the morning, Mark came into my office and asked me the same question. Not what the hell was wrong with me, but what was wrong with Hawn and how was I doing? I told him she broke her leg. I explained what the vet had done, and that she was recovering nicely. As we were talking, I spotted Malcolm coming in. He stood looking into my office for a full minute before going up to the teller.

"Are you alright? You're white as a ghost," Mark said, leaning forward. Then he looked around to see what I was looking at and spotted Malcolm. Frowning, he turned back to me. "Sally, please remember that if you ever need anything at all, I'm ready to help you." He stood up, waiting for me to respond.

"Thank you, Mark. I appreciate it."

He nodded and walked out of the office, making a point of closing my door behind him. I immediately picked up the phone and tried to appear to be in conversation with someone, while making notes on a pad on my desk. Malcolm finished with the teller and walked towards my office, then turned around and left. I felt physically sick. I hurried into the restroom and just made it to the toilet, where I threw up. Betty came in behind me.

"Sally? Are you okay?" she said, tapping on the door.

I came out and went straight to one of the sinks. Splashing cold water on my face.

"I'm okay. Thanks Betty."

"You don't look okay." She gave me a questioning look.

Suddenly, I couldn't hold it any longer. Tears poured down my face. I couldn't breathe for a second. She put her arms around me and just held me, saying nothing. Finally, I pulled myself together.

"If I tell you something, will you promise to not say a word to anyone?"

"Of course."

I told her the whole story. How Malcolm had beaten me back when we lived in Austin. About Caitlin's Escape Route, and how she helped me to get away and start again here. And how Malcolm had found me and convinced me he'd changed. He'd attended anger management. Finally, that he had kicked Hawn and broken her leg.

Betty listened without saying a word. Her forehead creased and her hand held to her mouth.

"Oh, Sally! That's terrible. I'm so sorry. What're you going to do now?"

"I don't know. I know I should tell him to leave. But—I can't."

"Or maybe you're afraid to? Are you afraid that he'll hurt you again?"

I thought about that for a minute. "I don't know. Maybe I'm just not ready." I took a deep breath. "Thanks for listening Betty. It really helps to have someone to talk to about it."

"Anytime you want to talk. I'm here."

She walked with me back to my office and sat down, making small talk for a few more minutes. I think she was making sure I really was alright.

~~

Malcolm said nothing about his visit to the bank. I had half expected him to start on again about Mark. But he didn't. He was on his best behavior for the rest of the week. Helping with setting the table and stacking the dishwasher again.

On Friday evening, he suggested we go somewhere in the camper for the weekend.

"No. Thanks. I'm not feeling very well. I think I'll just have a quiet weekend and rest."

"What's wrong? Do you need to see a doctor?" He actually sounded concerned.

"Oh, I don't think it's anything serious. I'll be fine if I just rest. Probably working too hard." I was going to say, probably the shock of

Hawn's surgery, but stopped myself just in time. That would have irritated him, and I didn't need to do that.

~~

Next morning, I was feeling much worse. As soon as I'd had breakfast, I started throwing up again. By lunchtime I realized I needed to see the doctor. Fortunately, there was a Saturday clinic that took walk-ins. I had difficulty convincing Malcolm that he should stay home, finally saying I needed him to keep an eye on Hawn.

It was a packed waiting room. I had to wait for almost two hours. Finally, a physician's assistant called me. She explained that if she thought I needed to see the doctor, she would redirect me, but if she could help me, I could get out faster. That worked for me.

After questioning me about my symptoms, doing the usual blood pressure and temperature checks. She handed me a small glass bottle and told me to go next door to the restroom and come back with a sample.

When I handed her the bottle, I watched as she stuck a cardboard strip into it. Pulled it out and waved it gently. Then she checked it and looked at me with a wide grin.

"Mystery solved, my dear. Congratulations. You're pregnant."

I sat there staring at her. "Wha—What?" I squeaked. "Pregnant?"

"Yes, you know. Going to have a baby."

"Oh, God! No!" I burst out crying.

"Apparently, you hadn't planned this?"

"No. I didn't, and it couldn't have come at a worse time," I said, wiping my eyes.

She shuffled papers around on her desk and then handed me a bunch of leaflets.

"Okay, this is all the information you need for right now. Leaflets on local family planning clinics if you decide on a termination. Adoption information if you prefer to go that route. And finally, proper pregnancy care. You'll need to see the doctor sometime soon, no matter what you decide. So, make an appointment on your way out."

~~

"Well? What did the doctor say?" Malcolm said as soon as I opened the door to the apartment.

I took the leaflets out of my purse. Walked into the kitchen and stood there staring at him in silence for what seemed like a long time. Then I walked over to the couch and dropped the leaflets on it.

"What? Is it something serious?" He actually looked genuinely concerned.

"I'm pregnant," I said. Sitting down suddenly as it finally sank in.

A few months ago, I would have been delighted. Today, it was the worst news I could imagine. I looked up at Malcolm. The look on his face said it all. He couldn't have grinned more widely, nor looked more pleased.

"A baby! Our baby! That's the best news I've had since I found that bank newsletter."

He didn't seem to notice that I was not sharing his excitement. He gathered up cushions and put them behind me. Brought over a low stool, put a cushion on it and told me to put my feet up.

"Now, what can I get you? No alcohol, of course. Would you like some water or lemonade? Hot tea?"

I just stared at him. I wasn't even sure he knew how to make hot tea.

"A glass of water would be good, thanks." I pointed to the leaflets on the couch. "These are our options," I said.

He brought me a glass of water, picked up the leaflets, and sat down beside me.

"Abortion! No way." He looked at me with absolute horror. "Adoption? Not going to happen." He crumpled up those two and threw them across the room, toward the wastepaper basket.

"It's okay. I agree. I've made an appointment to see the doctor for next week."

Malcolm hovered around me while I prepared dinner, trying to help. He set the table and, after dinner, insisted that I sit down while he cleared the table and tidied up. Maybe this was what he needed to jerk him back on track. I hoped so, because I didn't want to think about a future with him, and a baby, if he was going to be abusive. It would be impossible to kick him out. I shuddered as I thought about it.

"Are you cold? Can I get you anything?" I don't think I had ever seen him look so concerned.

"No, thanks. I'm fine. Just tired."

For the rest of the evening, Malcolm fussed over me. He even took care of Hawn, taking her out for a short walk and settling her down for the night. I just hoped that this would last.

"Are you going to tell Bill and Vickie tomorrow?" he asked me, as we headed to bed. Once again, he was back in my bed. I didn't argue. He was my baby's father.

"No. I don't want anyone to know until I make it to the four-month mark."

"Why?" he asked, frowning.

"Because a lot of women miscarry a first pregnancy in the first trimester. You don't hear about it because they don't tell anyone they're pregnant. It is fairly normal."

"Oh, I hope that doesn't happen!"

I paused. "In fact, I think I'll text Aunt Vickie and cancel tomorrow. I can say it's because of Hawn's leg."

"Okay, anyway, you need the rest."

CHAPTER TWENTY-THREE

Thankfully, the morning sickness subsided and didn't interfere with my normal working day. As the weekend approached, I talked to Malcolm about what to do about brunch. I was worried that if I refused a mimosa, that would alert Aunt Vickie. We decided I should accept it, and Malcolm would ask for just orange juice. He could say he was driving later. But at some point, Malcolm would switch our drinks. It seemed like an unnecessary and elaborate plan, but I really didn't want to tell anyone that I was pregnant. Even though the only person who knew that Malcolm had become more abusive was Betty—I knew, and it embarrassed me.

I took the afternoon off work on Friday and Malcolm came with me to the doctor. I had a full checkup. The doctor said that all was well and gave me the information to arrange for an ultrasound as I approached the fourth month. He confirmed I was currently at between eight and ten weeks.

~~

I tried to believe Malcolm was returning to the good Malcolm. That somehow my pregnancy and the prospect of being a father had jolted him back to reality. I was almost thankful that I had not asked him to leave. Though every time I looked at poor Hawn's leg, I did pause and wonder if he would ever be the man I wanted him to be. I was still prepared to give him a chance. A child needs to have two parents.

The following week, something shattered my hopes and finally made me face reality. Once again, Malcolm was waiting outside the bank for me. I could not convince him that, not only did I prefer to walk, but it was also good for me. I sighed and got in the car.

"Who's that?" He snapped, pointing across the street.

I looked and was just in time to see Sam disappear behind a car in the parking lot, complete with a camera and zoom lens around his neck.

"Oh, for heaven's sake. That's Sam—the guy who was stalking me."

Before I could stop him, Malcolm was out of the car. Horns blared as he ran across the road. Sam's truck pulled out of the parking lot without stopping and took off amidst more horn blowing.

Malcolm got back in the car and slammed the door before turning and glaring at me.

"Did you know he was there? Did he come here to see you? Is that why you didn't want me to pick you up?"

"Oh, please Malcolm. No. I didn't see him. I didn't know he was there. I already told you I reported him to the police!"

He started up the engine and drove home in silence.

All evening, I could see he was attempting to control himself. I believed he was using whatever he'd learned in anger management to stay calm and be rational. Despite that, I was very nervous. I was glad when it was time to go to bed. I hoped he'd forget about it.

After that, Malcolm was outside the bank every evening. I decided that there was no point in arguing. After a week, he started coming into the bank and depositing any cash he'd made in tips that day. I knew it was an excuse to see what was going on. To watch me. But I let it go because I knew there was nothing for him to see and maybe he'd realize that and stop being so suspicious.

I didn't really notice that he always seemed to go to Amanda until one morning, as I was getting coffee, when Mark came in immediately followed by Amanda.

"Good morning, all," she said. I wasn't used to her being quite so cheery.

"Good morning," I responded.

Mark just nodded, taking a sip of his coffee.

"Oh, and congratulations Sally. Malcolm told me your good news!"

Mark was just leaving the kitchen and paused.

"What's that?" he said.

"Didn't she tell you? Oh, I hope it isn't a secret? She's expecting." She looked delighted with herself.

I was furious. How could he have told her? I couldn't believe it.

"Well, it's not so much a secret. But I've told no one yet. I was waiting for the second trimester to go public."

I took my coffee back to my office and closed the door. My heart was pounding. I was so angry. As I thought about it, I realized Malcolm had told Amanda, knowing that she would not keep it to herself. No doubt he felt the knowledge that I was pregnant would ensure that Mark kept his distance. Obviously, he would anyway, but it seemed to be impossible to convince Malcolm. I stood up and caught Betty's eye, signaling to her to come in.

As I was telling her what had just happened, her expression darkened. She clenched her jaw. I half expected to hear her teeth grinding.

"I can't believe he told her. I believe she did that, though. No doubt that's exactly why he told her. What are you going to do?" she said, shaking her head.

I sighed. "I don't know what to do. As soon as I told him, he was thrilled. He started being so caring and kind again. It didn't last long, though. He's going back to being suspicious again." I told her about him chasing after Sam. "I don't know what to do."

"Well, if there's anything I can do to help you, let me know."

~~

That evening, as I got in the car, I asked Malcolm why he'd told Amanda.

"We agreed we wouldn't tell anyone. Besides, I wanted Aunt Vickie to be the first person to know."

"Sorry about that. It slipped out. I didn't mean to say it." He looked pleased with himself.

"Well, let's go tell her now. I certainly don't want her to hear from anyone else."

"Okay," Malcolm said as he drove in that direction.

"This is a lovely surprise. What are you doing here on a weekday evening?" Aunt Vickie said as she opened the door to us.

When I told them why we were there, Aunt Vickie clasped her hands together and looked like a child at Christmas. Uncle Bill congratulated Malcolm and hugged me. It seemed to me his hug was a little tighter and longer than necessary. As he stepped back, he turned away quickly, as Aunt Vickie started asking all the usual questions.

I answered her questions and then said we had to get home to let Hawn out. Promising to be there for Sunday brunch, as usual.

When we finally sat down after dinner, Malcolm wanted to know what Amanda had said.

"She just congratulated me in front of everyone," I said, doing my best to keep my tone even.

"Well, that was okay then, right?"

"She said nothing nasty, if that's what you mean. I just would have preferred for them not to know yet."

"But why? Are you embarrassed by it? They're going to know soon enough." There was a slight edge to his voice as he furrowed his brow.

"No, of course not. But it's just a superstition not to tell anyone before the fourth month."

Thankfully, he said nothing more about it. Also, he hadn't mentioned Sam again. I hoped he'd forgotten about him.

CHAPTER TWENTY-FOUR

Next morning, it surprised me that Malcolm was up and ready to go at the same time as I was.

"Got an early start today?" I asked him.

"No. From now on I'm going to drive you to work in the morning. If that Sam guy's still hanging around, you're not safe walking. Besides, I worry about you walking. What if the sidewalks are icy?"

I could see from his face that it would be foolish to argue. He clenched his jaw and stood at the door, frowning at me, as though he were just waiting for me to object.

"Okay. Thanks." A fleeting look of disappointment rewarded me.

Of course, I wasn't happy. But I was learning to pick my fights. In fact, I would prefer to avoid fighting at all costs. What I wasn't prepared for was for him to get out of the car and walk me to the door of the bank. Luckily, he couldn't come in because it was closed to the public for another thirty minutes. I realized he probably would have come in otherwise. That was an uncomfortable thought. If he were going to insist on driving me, I better be this early every morning.

~~

After that, each day, Malcolm dropped me off in the morning and picked me up in the evening. He didn't bother getting out of the car once he realized he couldn't actually walk me into the bank. I know he would have if he could.

Two weeks after the incident with Sam outside the bank, we saw him again. This time, he was climbing into his truck across the road from our apartment and pulled away. Malcolm jumped out of the car, leaving the driver's door open, and rushed to the street. There was no sign of Sam or his truck. I locked up the car and went inside to see to Hawn. I didn't want to be anywhere near Malcolm at that moment.

He came stomping into the apartment, slamming the front door behind him.

"How the fuck did he know where you live?" He yelled. When Hawn started growling, he lowered his voice. "Well?"

"I told you I went out with him a few times. Naturally, he knows where I live."

"Ha! So, is he the father of that bastard you're carrying?" he said, pointing at my belly.

"How can you think such a thing? This is your child. How can you speak about your own child like that?" I sat down on the couch and put my face in my hands. I guess pregnancy had taken away my self-control because I started crying. Hawn came over and put her head in my lap, nudging my hands. Malcolm glared at me, came towards me, then looking at Hawn, he turned around and left. A few seconds later, I heard the car start up.

"Thank you, Hawn," I said, stroking her head.

I was already in bed when Malcolm finally got home. His dinner was in the microwave. I guess he found it because it was gone the next morning. He drove me to work in silence and pulled away, almost before I got out of the car.

That evening, he arrived at the bank before closing, and sat on the chair outside my office. I noticed Betty glancing at him with a frown. Eventually, she stood up and headed to my office with a large binder in her hands.

"Do you have a minute to discuss this account?" she said as she stuck her head around the door.

"Sure, come in." I didn't know what account she was referring to.

She closed the door and put the binder on my desk before sitting down.

"I just wanted him to think I'm here to talk business. Are you okay?"

"Yes, thanks. I'm fine. Sam has been hanging around again, so I guess Malcolm is being paranoid." I smiled, hoping to reassure her. It was nice to know that she had my back.

She nodded, and leaning forward, she opened the binder and went through the pretense of discussing something in it.

"Let me know if there's anything I can do to help," she said, picking up the binder and walking back to her desk.

I hurriedly got ready to leave before security started closing the doors; I was still too late to stop Amanda from waylaying us as we headed for the door.

"Hello, Malcolm. Nice to see you," she said.

"Hi. Sorry, we're in a hurry this evening." He sounded like he was attempting to be polite as he took my elbow and steered me out of the bank.

For once, I didn't mind him taking control.

The drive home was as silent as the drive to work had been. Though he seemed to be a little more relaxed, he still gripped the steering wheel tightly and kept glancing down every side street we passed.

When we got home, thankfully, there was no sign of Sam. I took Hawn's leash from its hook in the hall. Surprised that she wasn't there to greet us, I went into the kitchen, calling to her.

I searched everywhere, then went out to the tiny patio area at the back. Perhaps Malcolm had left her out there. Still no sign.

"Malcolm." I called. "When did you last see Hawn?"

"This morning, when we left," he said, coming in the front door. "Why?"

"I can't find her. She's gone!"

"How can she be gone? Look out on the patio. Perhaps we left her there?"

"You just said you saw her here when we left this morning. Anyway, I looked outside. I looked everywhere." I could feel my stomach tighten and my heart racing. Sitting down, I took a few deep breaths.

"I've got to go out and search for her. She can't have gone far with her leg the way it is." I said, standing up again and heading for the front door.

"Let me help you."

He disagreed when I suggested we split up. He was still afraid that Sam was around somewhere. For three hours we searched the neighborhood and the dog park, calling her name and whistling. By the time we got home, I was exhausted and miserable. I sat on the couch and cried. Malcolm sat beside me and put his arms around me.

"How could she have gotten out?" I said, when I could cry no more.

"Perhaps someone stole her?"

"How? We didn't set the alarm, but the doors and windows were all locked."

"Maybe the landlord came, and she escaped when he opened the door? Or perhaps your stalker climbed over the back wall and got the back door open somehow?"

I shook my head. "I don't know. In the morning I'll make up fliers to hang around the area. Perhaps someone has found her and is taking care of her."

"Good idea. Now, how about I call in a pizza? It's late, and you're too tired to cook."

I nodded. At least he wasn't angry anymore. That was one good thing.

~~

I got into work earlier than usual the next morning to give me time to create fliers. I had emailed myself a photo of Hawn and set to work putting something together. As I finished up, I spotted Mark going into the kitchen and went over to talk to him.

"Good morning, Sally." He paused and studied my face. "Are you okay?"

I guess the hours of crying had left their mark.

"Yes, well, actually no. Hawn disappeared yesterday."

"Your dog? That's awful."

"I wanted to check with you—would it be alright to print out some fliers?"

"Of course, go right ahead. Good idea. Put one on the notice board, too."

"Thanks." I headed back to my office and seconds later was standing by the printer waiting for the fliers to finish printing. As I watched them sliding into the tray, I thought about what Malcolm had said. I couldn't believe that Sam had stolen Hawn. He'd met her, and he loved animals. I just didn't believe he would break into my apartment and steal her. I hoped that whoever had her, they were taking good care of her.

Hopefully, someone has her, and she's not wandering the streets alone.

As soon as the doors shut for the evening, I gathered up my stack of fliers and headed out. Malcolm was waiting at the curb. At least he had stopped coming in to wait for me.

That evening, and every evening for the rest of the week, I went out and posted fliers around the neighborhood. Malcolm insisted on coming with me. I wasn't sure if he was being supportive or suspicious, but either way; I appreciated the help.

"This weekend we should go further afield, to the national parks and hang fliers," I said.

"That's just stupid Sally. There is no way she strayed that far."

"I know, but people from around here go visit those parks all the time. Perhaps someone who has her, or saw her, or knows someone who has her, would be at the park and see the fliers."

"No. Like I said, that's stupid and I will not go all over the State looking for her."

I wanted to argue with him, but I knew better. The look on his face was enough to shut me up. All day at work, and all evening after dinner, I kept checking my phone to see if anyone called to report seeing Hawn. Nothing.

~~

By the end of the week, Malcolm showed signs of losing his patience. Or perhaps stopped pretending to be supportive. After spending all day Saturday walking around the neighborhood and sitting at the dog park, searching for any sign of Hawn, he finally lost it.

"This has got to stop! Just accept that the dog's gone and get over it," he said as we sat down after dinner.

"I can't do that. I have to find her. She has to be somewhere. It's the middle of winter!"

"She is probably dead. You just need to grow up and accept reality."

"That's a horrible thing to say." I stood up, hoping that my feelings of contempt were not showing on my face.

"Don't you dare look at me like that," he yelled, standing up and taking a step towards me, his arm raised.

I jumped back, but not fast enough. He caught me a glancing blow across the mouth. I let out a scream and put my hand to my face. It came away covered in blood. I rushed into the bathroom and locked the door. As I held a wet towel to my face, trying to stop the bleeding. Malcolm hammered on the door.

"Open this fucking door now."

I didn't. I looked in the mirror at the damage. He had split my lip, and though I had stopped the bleeding, it was swelling. Suddenly, the door crashed open, and Malcolm almost fell into the room.

"You broke the damn door!"

He grabbed me by the arm and swung me around to face him. Glancing from the bloody towel in my hand to my face. Suddenly, the anger seemed to drain from his face.

"Yes. And I wonder what Uncle Bill will make of this tomorrow."

"Shit." He said, dragging me back into the living room. His eyes became slits as his face went red. I suddenly realized that I needed to shut up and avoid needling him.

He pushed me onto the couch and stood there staring at me, visibly shaking. Then he turned and almost ran out of the apartment. I sat there for a few minutes. I'd promised myself that I would make him leave if he ever hurt me again, but that was easier to say when he was not being abusive. Now I was afraid he would kill me if I told him to leave. I got up and looked at the bathroom door. There was a crack in the wood where he had kicked the door in, and the lock was bent. I would have to get someone to fix it. That would mean taking a day off work.

Later that evening, Malcolm came home with a bunch of flowers.

"I'm so sorry, Sal," he said, handing me the flowers. "Please forgive me?"

I took the flowers, and as I was putting them in a vase, he watched me in silence.

"Sal? I guess I was just stressed out over Hawn and everything. I sure didn't mean to hurt you. Let's just tell your uncle that you fell. We could say you tripped when you were trying to hang the fliers. Okay?"

I nodded. I was making my own plans, so it suited me to go along with him just for the moment.

CHAPTER TWENTY-FIVE

My lip had become swollen and red by Monday morning. There was no way to disguise it with makeup, so I just went with the story of the fall. It had worked the day before with Uncle Bill and Aunt Vickie. Though I saw a flicker of suspicion cross Uncle Bill's face as he looked from me to Malcolm. He said nothing. Aunt Vickie was concerned, but more taken up with worry about Hawn to pay a lot of attention once she established that no major damage had been done.

"Thank goodness you didn't break a tooth," was all she said.

When I got to the office, everyone asked me what had happened. I felt like posting a notice on the board. Naturally, I didn't. I just repeated the lie each time. Later in the morning, Betty came into my office, closing the door behind her. She sat down, studying my face for a few minutes in silence.

"So, what really happened? Did he hit you?"

I nodded, and as she opened her mouth, I held a hand up before she could say anything.

"I know. I said I would tell him to leave if he ever hurt me again. But when it happened, I realized I couldn't tell him to leave then. As angry as he was, he would probably have killed me. But I have a plan." I paused. "He kicked in the bathroom door—after he did this—I locked myself in the bathroom to get away from him, and to wash it. So now the door needs to be repaired."

"Okay, so what's the plan?"

"I'm going to have to get a carpenter to come and fix the bathroom door. Of course, I'll have to stay home for that. I'll get him to change the locks on the front and back doors at the same time." I sat back, waiting to see what she thought of my idea. She raised her eyebrows.

"What about your car? If you just lock him out, he might just go off with that? Or break down the front door?"

"Oh. That's true. I didn't think of that." I felt my stomach drop and took a few deep breaths, afraid I would start throwing up again. "What would you suggest?"

"How about you do what you were planning? I'll come over and spend the day with you. As soon as he gets home, you can ask him for the keys and tell him he needs to leave. You'll have the new locks anyway, so the keys are not so important. But you should get the keys to the car back. He won't attack you with a witness there."

"That's perfect! If you don't mind doing that?"

"Cool. It's a plan. As soon as you set up the carpenter, let me know and I'll take that day off, too."

Later that day, I messaged Betty that I had scheduled the door to be repaired and the locks changed for Friday morning.

Over dinner, I told Malcolm that I was taking Friday off.

"Why?" He frowned at me.

"I have a carpenter coming to fix the bathroom door."

"Oh. Okay." He quickly changed the subject.

~~

On Friday morning, Malcolm delayed leaving the apartment until the carpenter arrived. Luckily, he turned out to be an older man. Obviously satisfied that I was not planning on entertaining another man, he headed out to work. Betty had agreed to join me for lunch.

As expected, the carpenter finished before she got there. He had fixed the bathroom door, though the paint needed to be touched up. Both the front and back doors had new locks fitted. I would let the landlord know about that after I had dealt with Malcolm.

By the time Betty arrived, I'd made a salad, freshly baked bread and a jug of iced tea. Over lunch, we discussed the best way to approach things when Malcolm got home.

"He's going to know something is up when his key doesn't work on the front door." Betty said.

"I never thought of that! You're right. I'll have to open the door to him, and he's going to be pissed."

"Well, I think he's going to be pissed, anyway. Nothing's going to change that. Should we both go to the door to let him in?"

I thought about that for a minute, chewing on a piece of bread.

"No. How about we leave the front door open? The weather's pleasant. That way, he'll walk in and close it behind him. He'll probably complain about it being open, but that's nothing compared to how he'll complain when I tell him to leave."

"Okay, that sounds like a good plan. What time would you expect him home?"

"I have no idea. He'll probably try to be early as it's Friday and he'll worry about me being here without supervision."

"I don't know how you can live with that." Betty shook her head slowly, her forehead creased.

"I can't. It's been awful. The first few weeks after he turned up—I was very nervous. I didn't believe he could change. Slowly, he convinced me—I really thought he'd changed. Now it's just like it used to be. Except worse because I can't keep running. But this time I know he won't stop; he can't change. He's just going to get worse."

After we cleared the table. I went to the front door. As I opened it, Malcolm was standing outside, poised to put his key in the lock.

"Where were you going?" He snapped at me.

"Nowhere. I thought I heard something at the door. I was hoping it was Hawn."

As we entered the kitchen, Betty stood up.

"What the hell is she doing here?" He glared at her and dumped the car keys on the counter. Betty picked them up quietly as he turned away.

"She came over for lunch. And to give me moral support."

"Moral support for what?"

"You need to leave." I picked up the small suitcase containing all of his things and handed it to him. "Get out. I'm done with you." Betty stepped forward and stood beside me.

He looked at us, his eyes bulging as a red flush spread from his neck up his face. His mouth formed into a snarl as he took the suitcase and hurled it at us. It knocked us both sideways.

Betty fell, hitting her head on the marble counter-top and dropped to the floor. I toppled sideways and lost my balance, sitting down hard on the floor.

Before I could move, he was on top of me. Punching and kicking. I tried to crawl away from him. He followed me, still kicking. I got under the table before blacking out.

When I came round, I was staring up at the underside of the table, wondering where I was. Suddenly, I remembered what had happened as I caught sight of Betty lying in a pool of blood on the floor. There was no sign of Malcolm. I pulled myself out from under the table and spotted my phone on the floor beside the couch. It took an enormous effort, but I crawled over to it and hit speed dial.

"Aunt Vickie," I said as soon as she picked up. My voice came out in a squeak. I swallowed hard.

"Hello, who is that?" I heard her say.

"Aunt Vickie, it's me, Sally," I said with difficulty.

"What's wrong dear? You sound terrible? Are you okay?"

"No. Malcolm attacked me and my friend. She's unconscious and bleeding. Is he at your house? Is the camper still there?"

"Oh my God! Are you hurt?"

"Yes, he kicked and punched me. I blacked out. I don't know how long for."

"No, the camper is gone—Did you call for an ambulance?"

"No. I didn't think to—I guess I should."

"I'll call one and come over right away, dear. Hold on!"

I crawled over to Betty and checked her for a pulse. She was still alive. There was a nasty gash on the back of her head. She still had the car keys clutched in her hand.

I knew I was going to have to get to the front door and somehow open it before the ambulance arrived. I didn't even try to stand up. If I did, I was afraid I would collapse and not be able to get to the door at all. Half crawling and half dragging myself, I finally reached the front door. Using the table in the hall, I pulled myself to my feet and reached for the lock. As I opened it, my legs gave way, and I fell backwards. The door swung open, and Aunt Vickie rushed in. I heard sirens in the distance.

~~

I opened my eyes and tried to figure out where I was. I turned my head, but it hurt too much, so I stopped.

"Ah. You're awake. How are you feeling?" Aunt Vickie appeared above me, as though she were floating. I blinked hard. Then I realized I was lying down, and she was standing over me.

"Everything hurts."

Suddenly, it came back to me. The last thing I remembered was hearing sirens.

"Betty! How's Betty?" I said, struggling to sit up.

Aunt Vickie gently pushed me back on the pillow. "She's in the next ward and she's going to be fine. She took a nasty blow to the head and needed stitches. Most definitely, she has a concussion, but the doctor says she'll make a full recovery. Her parents are with her."

"Thank you so much, Aunt Vickie."

"Of course, my dear. Now you just get some rest."

I drifted in and out of sleep for the next few hours. At times a nurse was fiddling with the drip hanging to one side of my bed. At other times, I was alone.

I opened my eyes, finally feeling less like I was drifting. I looked around and there was Betty, sitting in the chair where Aunt Vickie had been. She was reading a magazine.

"Betty? Are you okay?"

She looked up and smiled.

"Yeah. That didn't work out quite like we planned. Did it?"

I started to shake my head and thought better of it.

"No. I'm so very sorry. If I thought he was going to hurt you, I would never have let you come over."

"It wasn't your fault. How're you doing?" She studied me for a few seconds. "You look like shit."

I laughed and then groaned. "Oh, don't make me laugh. That hurts."

A nurse came in. She stopped when she saw Betty.

"What are you doing out of bed? You're not supposed to be in here."

Betty got up, and the nurse took her arm and led her out, returning a few minutes later.

"How're you feeling?" she said as she checked the machines I appeared to be hooked up to.

"Sore all over."

"Not surprising. You've a couple of cracked ribs, a concussion and a few other minor injuries. The doctor will be in to see you in the morning and will discuss it all with you then. I'm putting a cocktail in your drip, so you should sleep now."

CHAPTER TWENTY-SIX

Next morning, Uncle Bill came in with Aunt Vickie.

"How're you feeling?" He asked me.

"A little better than yesterday, thanks. But I feel so foolish."

"He fooled us all, my dear. Thank goodness you're safe. The doctor says you'll be right as rain in no time."

"I haven't seen a doctor yet. He's supposed to come in to see me this morning."

"He'll be in shortly," Aunt Vickie said. "We spoke with him briefly as we were coming in. He's on his way."

"How's Betty?"

"Her parents are next door with her now. She's going to be discharged today." Just as Uncle Bill spoke, there was a knock on the door and Betty came in, followed by a couple she introduced to me as her parents.

"I'm so very sorry for what happened to Betty. It was entirely my fault and I feel so bad about putting her in such danger."

"We don't blame you at all, my dear. Betty told us the full story. It was not your fault," Betty's mother said.

"We just wanted to let you know that we've already told the police we want to press charges, and have that man charged with assault."

I nodded. "I'm surprised the police have not been to see me already."

"They will be. The doctor wouldn't let them near you yesterday. No doubt after he sees you today, they'll be in," Uncle Bill said. "And of course, you will press charges, too."

Minutes after Aunt Vickie and Uncle Bill left, there was another knock on the door. Before I could respond, a man with slicked back silver hair and a pair of glasses perched on the end of his nose came in. He introduced himself as Dr. Lee; he looked like he had stepped out of a hospital series on TV.

"How're you feeling this morning?" he said, standing in front of the small computer mounted on the wall. He swiped his card and peered at the screen in silence for a few minutes. Then he perched on the side of the bed, making sure not to sit on my feet. Looking at me over the top of his glasses, waiting for my response.

"Everything hurts still, but I'm feeling better than I did yesterday. Thank you." I was beginning to think I should make a sign that says 'Everything Hurts' and just hold it up when anyone asked me how I was doing.

He nodded. "You took a hell of a beating. It's surprising that you have no broken bones apart from a few ribs."

"Dr.—what about my baby?" I'd been afraid to ask anyone up to now.

His eyebrows gathered up in a frown. "So far, so good. But you're not out of the woods yet. On the good side, your baby is doing okay; the bad news is that you were hemorrhaging heavily when they brought you in. The next few days will be critical, so we need you to have complete bed rest." He stood up and replaced the chart. "Be sure and call a nurse if you get any stomach pain at all, or if you notice any sign of blood." He waited to be sure I'd heard him. I stared at him, nodding. He patted my shoulder. "Try not to worry and just rest. Okay?" Nodding again, I watched him leave the room.

Leaning back against the pillows, all I could think of was what a mess I had made of my life. Letting Malcolm into my life, not once, but a second time, when I already knew what he was like. How stupid could I be? Wasting all the effort that Caitlin and Pat had put into helping me escape from him the first time. I not only invited him back in. I got pregnant. Of course, I wanted this baby, but it would tie me to Malcolm forever.

I'd lost Hawn. Malcolm proved he had not changed, and now I risked losing my baby.

~~

Another knock on the door interrupted my thoughts. I looked up, waiting for someone else to come in. Another softer knock.

"Come in." I called.

A head appeared around the door. Mark! He studied me for a few seconds.

"Sally?"

I guess Malcolm had battered my face worse than I thought, and I know my hair was a mess.

"Yes, it's me."

He came in and placed an enormous bunch of flowers on the table beside me, handing me a card.

"From everyone at the bank," he said. "How are you? You look—" He paused. "You look—sore."

"Yeah, it is sore. I'm better than I was yesterday. Thanks for the flowers and for coming in."

"Not at all. I'm terribly sorry about what happened to you and Betty. I just can't believe it."

"Poor Betty. She was just there to help me. We thought he would do nothing with her there."

"What happened? If you don't mind me asking?"

I told him about my history with Malcolm, how he'd tracked me to Cambridge, and convinced me that anger management had changed him.

"He kicked Hawn and broke her leg when she attempted to protect me."

"Do you think her disappearance has something to do with him?"

"I tried to believe he would not do such a thing. But I'm convinced now that he got rid of her." I'd been trying not to cry, but the thought of Hawn was too much.

Mark handed me a tissue and patted my hand. "As soon as you're better, we'll go searching for her. If he got rid of her, then you'll need fliers much further afield. He probably drove out into the countryside, or one of the national parks, and left her there. We'll find her."

"Thank you."

He stayed another hour and promised to be back the following day.

"Let me know if there's anything you need," he said as he left.

The nurse came in and fiddled around with the monitors, injected another cocktail of medications into my drip, and left. I drifted off to sleep.

I woke up with a crippling pain in my back. It was dark. Remembering the doctor's instructions, I grabbed the call bell and pressed the button. A few minutes later, a nurse came in.

"You rang the bell. Are you alright?"

I gasped as a pain in my stomach caused me to draw my knees up. She hurried over to me. The rest of that night was a blur. They whisked me off to what I presume was an operating theater. And thankfully, I remember nothing more until I woke up back in my room. It was daylight, and Aunt Vickie was in the chair beside my bed again.

"I lost the baby, didn't I?"

"I'm so sorry. Yes, I'm afraid they couldn't save her." Aunt Vickie reached over and squeezed my hand.

"Her? It was a girl?" I wanted to cry, but somehow, I was empty.

That evening, Mark came in again. He stayed about an hour, and once again promised we would go searching for Hawn as soon as they discharged me.

~~

The following day, a nurse ushered two police officers into my room. I described the camper, gave them the registration details, and said that I believed he would camp somewhere close by. They told me that Malcolm had picked up his camper without being seen the evening of the assault and then emptied his bank account.

They said that they would search all the surrounding camping areas and wanted to know if I thought he would go back to Texas. Somehow, I was sure he would hang around, either to get back with me, or to hurt me again. They questioned me for almost two hours.

By the time they left, I was exhausted. They assured me they would do everything they could to track Malcolm down and he would pay for what he had done.

CHAPTER TWENTY-SEVEN

The hospital discharged me three days later, with instructions to take it easy for another week before returning to work.

Aunt Vickie picked me up, and she and Uncle Bill insisted I stay with them for that week. I didn't put up much of an argument. I spent the next week being fussed over.

After brunch on Sunday, I walked home. I was due to go back to work the next day.

"Let me drive you home, my dear," Uncle Bill said.

"Thanks, but I would prefer to walk. I need the exercise."

"I have some groceries for you, just a few things in case you need them." Aunt Vickie gave me a canvas grocery bag.

"That is so thoughtful." I hugged them both and left.

As soon as I started walking, I felt as though emptiness surrounded me. No Hawn. While no Malcolm was a good thing—I couldn't help but check down every street and around every corner as I walked, for fear he was suddenly going to appear. Still, I felt like something was missing. I guess it was the dream that I missed. I finally had to face the fact that he was just bad, and nothing would change that. Perhaps I needed to stop dreaming and face reality.

As I approached my front door, Gina was coming out of their basement apartment.

"Hi Sally. We heard you were in the hospital. How're you doing?"

"Recovering, thanks," I said, hoping they didn't know the details.

"Good to hear it. It was lucky your friend was able to keep an eye on your apartment while you were gone."

"Who?"

"You know, the guy with the camper who was staying with you? I saw him checking on the place one day—about ten days ago when you were in the hospital, anyway. I tried to get his attention to ask him how you were, but he seemed to be in a hurry."

"Camper…" My legs felt like they were going to give way. I reached out to grab hold of my car for support.

"Are you okay? You're very pale. Here, let me help you to your door."

"I'm good thanks Gina." But I let her take my groceries and my elbow. I didn't want to fall on my face in front of her.

I opened the door, and I took the bag from her. "Thank you. Sorry for being such a wimp." I tried to smile.

"Not at all. Are you sure you're okay?" Her face creased with concern.

"I'm fine, honestly. Thanks."

As I stepped into the hallway and closed the door behind me, I felt anything but fine. A foul smell caught at the back of my throat, and I felt like gagging. It seemed to come from the kitchen. I was almost afraid to go in. Slowly, I stuck my head around the door with my hand clamped over my nose and mouth. I don't know how long I stood transfixed, staring. The kitchen was a disaster. The fridge door hung open, and it looked like everything had been pulled out and dumped on the floor. There was food thrown everywhere. Sugar, flour, bread, smashed eggs, even milk poured out and gone sour. Then I noticed the walls were covered in spray paint. Someone had written obscenities all over the walls and even on the ceiling.

Malcolm! It must have been. Gina said she saw the camper.

I grabbed my phone and called Uncle Bill.

"Hey Sal. Are you safe home?"

"Uncle Bill!" I couldn't say anything else. There was a lump in my throat and a pressure on my lungs, preventing me from taking a breath.

"Sally! What's wrong?"

"Uncle Bill," I repeated, trying to breathe normally without inhaling the awful smell was impossible. I started to gag again. Running out of the kitchen, I pulled open the front door and took a deep breath of clean air. "My apartment—I think Malcolm was here and trashed it while I was in the hospital," I said, sitting on the steps.

"We'll be right over. Stay where you are."

Two hours later, we were back at Uncle Bill's. He called the police as soon as he saw my kitchen. Apparently, someone, we presume Malcolm, had broken in the back door. Not only was there rotting food all over the kitchen, and spray paint on the walls and ceiling, but there was also human waste on the countertops.

Aunt Vickie had contacted a cleaning company, and they were scheduled to start work on it the following morning. She was also going to arrange to have the back door fixed and the kitchen repainted.

"Looks like I'll be staying here for a while longer," I said.

"We are delighted to have you. I just wish it wasn't under such horrible circumstances," Aunt Vickie said. "I can't believe that we tried to like that man!"

~~

As I expected, Monday at work was difficult. Most of the day was taken up with explaining to my colleagues what had happened and how I was feeling. Although I knew Betty had already told them. Finally, they left me alone. It was going to take me the rest of the week to catch up with my work. But first, I picked up the phone and called Rick's office. I made an appointment for the following day. I would have to take a long lunch, but it was time to return to therapy before I made another awful mistake.

That evening, instead of walking directly back to Uncle Bill's after work. I took a roundabout route, hoping to spot Hawn, and at least checking the fliers were still in place. Quite a few were gone, so I replaced them.

As the daylight faded, I headed back to Uncle Bill and Aunt Vickie's.

Aunt Vickie confirmed that the cleaning crew were working on the kitchen, and she had asked them to give the entire apartment a thorough clean, just in case Malcolm messed up outside of the kitchen. They were going to finish up the following day. She had scheduled the painters to come in immediately after that, and the back door had already been repaired.

"It was definitely Malcolm," I said. "I checked the video online and you can clearly see him. He parked the camper up against the wall, climbed on the roof and used that to get over it."

I spent the rest of the evening working on various routes to take each evening in my search for Hawn. I was fairly certain it was a waste of time, but I had to try. I couldn't give up on her. There was still a possibility that someone in the immediate neighborhood had found her and taken her in, I had to keep searching. It was freezing cold. I hated the idea that Hawn might be out in this weather more than I feared Malcolm; I was determined that he would not stop me from searching for her.

~~

I drove to work the next morning. I didn't want to waste time getting to and from my therapy appointment.

Even though I knew Rick would not judge me, that's not how therapy works; still, I couldn't help feeling embarrassed. I had to force myself to get in the car and drive. As I parked in the small tarmac area in the front yard of the house where he had his office, I wanted to turn and run. I didn't.

Once again, I lay prone on that awful couch. Although that hour was difficult, it was also cleansing. I listened to myself recount all that had happened since my last visit. It horrified me to hear the incredibly stupid decisions I'd made. How did I not see it at the time?

Rick listened quietly, only saying something to prompt me when I stopped talking. The hour was almost up by the time I finished.

"I can't believe I made so many stupid decisions. What was I thinking?"

"Ah. That's very good. You are well on the way to getting back on an even keel. Recognizing where you went wrong is the key, and you have found it."

I was so surprised I sat up and looked at him. It sounded like he was paying me a compliment.

"You really think so? I'm so terrified to trust my own judgment. I can't go through all that again. My poor little baby." I couldn't hold back the tears.

Rick passed me a box of tissues and sat quietly, saying nothing. Finally, I took a deep breath and stood up.

"I'm sorry, look at the time!"

"No problem, Sally, this is what therapy's designed to do. The only way to move forward is to let go of the past. The only way to let go of the past is to face it and accept it for what it was and then let it go.

Sally's Story

That is exactly what you are doing. You're a very brave young woman. I'll see you at the same time on Thursday."

His words replayed in my head as I drove back to work, and all afternoon as I tried to clear my desk.

~~

Aunt Vickie had worked magic, and by Friday evening, my apartment was ready for me to move back. She had even restocked the fridge and pantry.

I was just getting ready to leave work when Mark came into my office.

"Hey, glad I caught you."

"I was just leaving. What's up?"

"I wanted to arrange for our search for Hawn tomorrow. I mentioned it while you were in the hospital." He studied me with his eyebrows up and his head to one side, clearly not sure if I remembered.

"I remember, and I really appreciate it, if you have the time. It is difficult to drive and search at the same time."

"Great! How about I pick you up at about ten tomorrow morning?"

"I'll be ready."

I was looking forward to the next day. Naturally, I wanted to find Hawn, but it would also be nice to not be alone. That thought was disconcerting, given my feelings about dating someone I worked with. So far, I'd been wrong in most of my assumptions. I was tired of trying to make things happen. I wasn't very good at that, anyway. Perhaps it was time to just go with the flow. Besides, it wasn't a date.

Uncle Bill had insisted that I should have dinner with them that evening, and then they would drive me back to my apartment. He was determined to ensure that I was safe there before they left me alone. I was happy to comply because after my last experience; I didn't want to go into the apartment alone, not until I was certain that it was safe to do so.

CHAPTER TWENTY-EIGHT

I was waiting at the doorstep when Mark pulled in.

"Sorry. Am I late?"

"No. I'm early. As usual."

"Okay, where to?"

"I would really like to go further afield, like to some of the national parks. I know that lots of people from around here go there on weekends. Many bring their dogs to walk the trails. There might be people who have seen Hawn or know someone who has her."

"Absolutely, I agree. And if Malcolm tried to get rid of her, he would have dumped her as far away as possible. Let's go!"

We drove for three hours, stopped for lunch, and then pulled into the parking area of a huge forest park. There was a visitors' center at one end of the parking lot. We asked them if they would mind posting one of my fliers. The woman behind the counter took it from me.

"It should be easy to identify this poor dog with that thing on its leg," she said as she pinned the flier to the notice board.

"Thank you," I said.

We spent about forty minutes walking around where there were people walking dogs. None of them looked like Hawn. In fact, there were no golden retrievers among them.

"Come on, we have time to hit one more park before we head home." Mark tried to sound cheerful, but I was fast losing hope of ever finding her. I guess I had half expected to drive into the park and see her sitting there waiting for me.

The visitors center at the second park was as helpful and took the flier. Once again, we did a quick walk around, but with no luck. Mark even stopped a few people and showed them the flier. No one remembered having seen Hawn.

We stopped for dinner on the way home.

"We'll go further afield next Saturday. We will find her," Mark said over dinner.

"Thank you. And I'll keep searching in my neighborhood each evening. There isn't much daylight time, but if someone local took her in, I just might see her."

"That's a good idea. I'll drive and you can search. We can cover more ground that way."

"If you're sure? I don't want to take up all your time."

"I'm certain. I'm on a mission now. Besides, you shouldn't be out on your own with Malcolm still free." He had a determined look on his face, so I didn't argue any more. I appreciated the help and the company.

~~

On Monday evening, Mark stuck his head around the door of my office.

"Ready to go? Let's get out of here now before anyone stops us."

"Sure, you're the boss." I glanced at my watch. It was still twenty minutes to closing time.

"We can get in a little more daylight searching this way." He held the door open for me. I glanced over my shoulder as I left and was relieved Amanda was nowhere to be seen.

We drove around the neighborhood in ever-widening circles for over an hour. As the sky darkened, a light misty rain started.

"We might as well give up," I sighed. "We won't find her in this."

"I guess you're right. Let's go grab something to eat and I'll drop you home. We can do this again every evening this week."

I said nothing. I wasn't sure what to say. But I didn't object. I was enjoying spending time with Mark, and it was so nice to have some company.

Every evening that week was a repeat. We slipped out a little early. Mark took a different route each time, and we covered a lot of ground but didn't see any sign of Hawn. Then we had dinner, and he dropped me home. By Friday, I was beginning to lose hope.

Sally's Story

"Don't give up Sally, I know we'll find her," Mark said as he pulled up outside my apartment.

"I'm sorry. I'm afraid I'm a bit dismal. But I really appreciate your help."

"You are actually great company. If this is you dismal, I'm looking forward to finding Hawn so that I can see you happy."

I could feel my face flushing, and turned to get out of the car before he noticed.

"I'll pick you up at ten in the morning?"

"That'd be great. Thanks again." I watched him drive off. I was looking forward to the next day. Naturally, I wanted to find Hawn, but I was also enjoying Mark's company.

~~

The following morning, Mark was waiting outside my apartment when I came out. It was a beautiful day, cold, but the sun was shining and there was no wind at all.

We drove to yet another park. This one was even further away. We repeated our process. As before, they took a flier and put it on the notice board and we walked around, asking anyone with a dog if they had seen Hawn. No one had.

As we were heading home, Mark pulled into one more park on the way. It was the same park where Malcolm and I had spent the day testing out the camper.

Again, we went first to the visitor's center, and I asked the woman behind the counter if she'd seen Hawn, and if she would post a flier.

"Certainly. I'll put it on the notice board," she said, studying it. "Hey, wait a minute—I saw a dog just like this a few weeks back. I thought it was odd."

"What was odd?" Mark asked.

"Well, this guy pulled up at the far end of the parking lot. He got out of his car with a dog who looked just like that." She pointed to the flier. "He walked around the area with her for about twenty minutes. Then he took her leash off, jumped into his car and drove away. I thought he was abandoning her because she was injured—she had something wrong with her leg."

"What happened to the dog?" I asked, holding my breath.

"That was the odd part. Another guy grabbed her collar and lifted her into his truck."

"What did the truck look like?" Mark and I asked in unison.

"It was an old truck, red and white, battered, kind of like a farm truck."

"I don't suppose you got the license plate number?" I had to ask, though I was sure she hadn't.

"No, even if I had thought to try, it was too far away for that—come to think of it, one of the security cameras might have caught it."

"Do you think we could see the video—and do you know how much history they have?"

"My son takes care of all that technical stuff. I know he keeps at least three months, and I'm sure he would be happy to let you see it. He's gone for today. Let me call him."

We watched as she disappeared into the office behind the counter. Mark put a hand on my shoulder and squeezed it gently. I realized I'd been holding my breath, terrified to hope. No doubt he could tell from my expression. I smiled at him and let out a sigh, trying to breathe normally and still afraid to believe we might have finally found her, or at least got a lead to where she might be.

"You're in luck," the woman said, as she came back to the counter. "He forgot something and is actually on his way back here now. He said he would be happy to go through the video with you."

"Thank you so much, by the way, my name's Sally, and this is Mark."

"Nice to meet you. I'm Heather and my son is Buddy. He should be here any minute now." She peered out the window towards the parking lot.

Ten minutes later, a truck pulled in and parked.

"There's Buddy now," Heather said.

As soon as introductions were done, Buddy brought us into a back room. We all sat down expectantly in front of a large computer screen as he fiddled with a collection of plugs and switches, finally sitting down at the keyboard as a video of the parking lot filled the screen.

"Approximately what date did your dog disappear?"

I gave him the exact date and approximate time. "It was sometime between nine in the morning and five in the evening."

He hit a key, and the video moved faster and then slowed down.

"Okay, this would be nine in the morning."

We all watch in silence as vehicles parked and people got out, some walking towards the visitors' center and some heading down the trail. Buddy fast forwarded in small sections.

"Just give a shout if you think you see your dog. We don't want to be here all night, so I'll keep it moving."

Five minutes later, I let out a yell. "There! Stop! That's my car, and that's Malcolm with Hawn!" As we watched, they started walking up and down the parking lot. "Heather said he walked her around for about twenty minutes. Can you jump a few minutes forward?"

"There?" Buddy moved the video forward and slowed down as we watched Malcolm remove the leash and jump into the car, pulling out of the parking lot fast. Almost immediately, an old red and white truck pulled out of a spot at the other end, up by the trail-head, and stopped beside Hawn. A man jumped out and picked her up and put her in the back seat, was back in the truck and pulling away within seconds.

"I swear that's Sam!"

"Who? You know him?" Mark said.

"Yes, Sam—the guy who has been stalking me."

Mark's eyebrows raised as he stared at me for a second. "Your stalker? Out here?"

"I know. It's totally weird. But I'm certain that's him."

"Can you contact him?"

In answer, I pulled out my phone.

"Hello? Sam? This's Sally. I believe you have my dog?"

"Oh, hey Sally. Yeah, I do. Why?"

"What do you mean, why? I want her back!"

"Oh, really? I thought you wanted your boyfriend to dump her because of her injury."

"Don't be stupid, of course I want her—what were you doing? Stalking Malcolm?"

"I just happened to be passing your apartment and saw your boyfriend put her in the car and drive off. I suspected he was up to no good, so I followed him."

"How is she? How's her leg?"

"Healing well. I took her to my vet, and he said she's almost ready to have the pins removed."

"Thank you for that. I'll refund you for the vet's bill and I'll be there to pick her up this evening."

"Sure. Looking forward to seeing you."

I disconnected and stood for a second, staring at the phone. I couldn't believe my ears. Then I looked at Mark. The look on his face matched exactly how I felt.

"Can you believe that? He had her all along! What an asshole—Oh, sorry. I never asked you if you would mind going to pick her up now?"

Mark grinned. "Indeed. I'll drive you to get her. I'd be delighted and I don't think it is a good idea for you to go there on your own."

I turned to Buddy, who was staring at me, his face a mixture of amusement and confusion. "Thank you so very much! I can't tell you how much I appreciate your help."

"Delighted to be able to help."

We said goodbye to Heather on our way out and almost ran to the car and headed back to Cambridge. I didn't realize that I'd been so stressed until I sat back and took a deep breath. For the first time in weeks, I felt I could breathe, I could relax.

CHAPTER TWENTY-NINE

The drive to Sam's seemed to take forever. We finally pulled up outside his house, and we both climbed out of the car and stretched. As we approached the front door, Sam opened it and Hawn came bounding out, nearly knocking me over. I got down on my knees beside her and buried my face in her soft coat. Mark went up to Sam and thanked him for taking care of her. On the way there, we had agreed that we would not mention the stalking, just get Hawn and leave.

We loaded her into the vehicle and drove off while Sam stood watching. He had refused my efforts to pay for his vet. I hoped that was the last I would see of him.

On the way home, I called Aunt Vickie to let her know I had found Hawn.

"That is wonderful news! Tell me all about it? How did you find her? Is she alright?"

"She's fine, and I'll tell you all about it over brunch tomorrow. I'm on my way home right now." I said as soon as I could get a word in. We pulled into my driveway as I hung up.

"What about dinner?" Mark said. "I know you don't want to go out tonight and leave Hawn alone. How about I go pick up something and bring it back?"

"That's a great idea! Thank you."

"Chinese or Indian, Italian? Thai? What would you prefer?"

"Chinese please."

"Okay, I'll be back in a few," Mark said as I unloaded Hawn.

When I opened the front door, Hawn dashed into the apartment and ran from room to room, sniffing everywhere. Her leg had obviously healed, and I would need to take her back to the vet on Monday. I put out a bowl of fresh water for her and watched as she lapped it up. I couldn't quite believe she was home.

By the time Mark returned with our dinner, I had set the table and put some food out for Hawn.

"I hope you like what I got," Mark said, pulling a variety of takeout containers from the bag he was carrying.

"I don't think there's any Chinese food that I don't like. You certainly got enough!"

"Well, I wanted to be sure there was something you would eat. You can save any leftovers for your dinner tomorrow."

After dinner, I stacked what remained in the fridge.

"I had better get going," Mark said, standing up. Before heading to the door, he turned to me and paused, studying me.

"What?" I said, wiping my mouth with a napkin. "Have I food on my face?"

He grinned. "No. I was just wondering, would you have dinner with me on Friday?" He said it so fast I wasn't sure I had understood him.

"Sorry? What did you say, dinner on Friday?"

"Yes. Now that we've found Hawn, I don't really have a good excuse to see you. Except that I enjoy your company and would love to continue doing so."

"Isn't there some rule about dating work colleagues? That sounds like a date, and I know some companies frown on it."

"I don't think so. I'll check. If there is, and you would agree to a date, I'll quit and get another job."

I couldn't help laughing at that. Mark chuckled, and suddenly we were both laughing helplessly. I guess it was partly hysteria on my part. After all that had happened, finally getting Hawn back was overwhelming. And it was thanks to Mark.

"Yes, I would love to have dinner with you on Friday." I said when I finally stopped laughing. "But please don't tell Amanda."

That set us off again. I couldn't remember the last time I had laughed so much or felt so happy.

"Get some sleep. See you on Monday." Mark said, and he left before I could answer.

I locked up, set the alarm, and went to bed.

~~

The next morning, I woke up with a smile on my face. I realized I had almost given up hope of ever finding Hawn.

Hawn was so excited to see Uncle Bill and Aunt Vickie that she exhausted herself by running around the garden, picking up sticks and depositing them at our feet. She finally collapsed in the shade of a tree and fell asleep.

"Who'd have thought you would be thankful for having a stalker?" Uncle Bill said, after I'd told them how we finally found Hawn.

"I know. That was my feeling too. But I should have known that Malcolm would want to get rid of her after she tried to protect me."

"Your boss sounds like a nice guy. That was very good of him, to help you find her." Aunt Vickie said.

"Yes." I thought about it for a moment, before continuing. I decided to tell them. "He asked me out to dinner on Friday. I said yes." I watched their faces, knowing that they were going to worry about me ever dating any man again.

"In that case, I think I would like to meet him." Uncle Bill said.

I couldn't help smiling. But I understood how he felt.

"I promise you, I'm taking this one slowly. I'll bring him to meet you if I decide to continue seeing him—assuming he wants to continue seeing me."

They still looked a little worried, but it was going to take us all a long time to recover from what Malcolm did—and my poor decisions.

CHAPTER THIRTY

On Monday morning, the first thing I did when I got into the office, even before making coffee, was to remove the flier from the notice board. As I walked into the kitchen, I had an idea. I took a green highlighter pen and wrote across the flier, FOUND!!!. Then I pinned it back on the board.

Throughout the day, as people noticed the flier update, there was great excitement. Betty came running into my office.

"You found her! That's so cool. Oh, I'm so happy for you." She hugged me and went running out again.

I could see Mark watching from outside his office with a grin on his face. Later in the morning, he came to my office with a bundle of papers, closing the door behind him. He handed me the papers with a serious look on his face; he pointed to them.

"Just pretend we are discussing work."

I had to look down to hide the smile on my face. "Okay. What are we discussing?"

"Friday. How about I pick you up at seven-thirty?"

"That sounds perfect. I can walk Hawn and be ready by then."

He stood up, nodding with a serious look on his face as he took the papers back.

"Looking forward to it."

"Oh, I'm going to leave early this afternoon. I need to take Hawn to the vet. Would that be okay?"

"Of course."

I watched him walk back to his office and caught sight of Amanda watching. Once again, I had to look down and busy myself with rearranging pens on my desk to hide the smile. No doubt if a relationship between me and Mark develops, she'll find out, but in the meantime, it amused me to watch her watching me.

Shortly after lunch, I packed up and headed home.

~~

I picked up Hawn and by two-thirty we were sitting in the vet's waiting room. There were assortments of cats in carriers, dogs and one rabbit, also in a carrier. It was almost three-thirty before they saw us.

It was clear from the x-ray that Hawn's leg had fully healed. They removed the contraption holding her leg together, and said they would keep her in overnight. I was to collect her the following afternoon. It was hard to leave her there, but comforting to know that she had finally healed.

Once again, the next day, I left work early to pick her up and together we went for a long walk.

The rest of the week went smoothly. Mark stayed away from my office unless there was actual business to discuss. Amanda continued to watch his every move. She was clearly worried that, with Malcolm out of the picture; I was once again competition. This time, she was correct.

Hawn and I got back into our evening routine, walking to the dog park and working on her obedience training. On Friday evening, as soon as we got back from our walk, I had a quick shower and took extra care doing my hair and makeup. I'd spent the entire week trying to decide what to wear. I settled on a full length, black silk skirt with a green silk blouse. It wasn't exactly the same as the one I had to throw away in Temple. In fact, it was nicer. I knew that green enhanced the color of my eyes, and silk seemed to make them sparkle.

At exactly seven-thirty, the doorbell rang. When I opened the door, Mark and I stood staring at each other for a few seconds before we both burst out laughing. He was wearing black chinos and a green shirt.

"Oh, dear." I gasped, attempting to stop laughing. "Perhaps I should change?"

"Absolutely not. You look gorgeous. I wore this green shirt because I thought it matched your eyes. I didn't mean to match your outfit, too."

Mark had made reservations at one of the better restaurants in the area. The dinner was amazing, and the service was excellent.

"Can we do this again soon?" Mark said as he pulled up outside my apartment.

"I would like that. I had a lovely evening, thank you."

"What are you doing tomorrow? Perhaps we could take Hawn and go to the beach. Have a picnic?"

"That sounds wonderful. I've no plans for tomorrow."

"Okay, you do now! I'll pick you up at ten."

He leaned across and kissed me. "Good night, Sally."

I started to say goodnight, but suddenly we were kissing again, our arms wrapped around each other. After a few minutes, I pulled back.

"Good night, Mark. See you tomorrow." I literally scrambled out of the car. I had promised myself that I was going to take things slowly. That was going to be more difficult than I had imagined.

Mark waited until I opened the front door before waving and pulling away.

CHAPTER THIRTY-ONE

When Mark arrived to pick us up on Saturday morning, once again, we looked at each other and couldn't stop laughing. We were both wearing light blue denim jeans and matching denim long-sleeved shirts.

"This is getting ridiculous," I said. "In future we need to plan what we wear, in advance."

"I like the sound of that—in the future." He smiled and then kissed me.

The weather was still not warm enough for the beaches to be crowded. We had it almost entirely to ourselves. Hawn loved the beach and the ocean. She barked and snapped at the waves, then rolled in the sand.

"Oh, no. She'll destroy your car with all that sand."

Mark just laughed. "She'll just shake it off once it dries. One thing's for sure, you won't need to walk her this evening."

I had never been in a relationship with someone like Mark. He was fun, caring and easy-going. I was beginning to believe we had a future, and I looked forward to it.

Mark was right, up to a point. Hawn dried off and shook out most of the sand. But when he dropped us off at the apartment that evening, and Hawn jumped out of the back seat, she left behind a layer of sand.

"It's not a problem, honestly. It's only sand and it'll vacuum up."

"Perhaps we should clean it now?"

"No, I'll get it done tomorrow. Don't worry."

"Well, if you say so. Would you like to come in? I know we stuffed our faces at the beach, but I could make something light for dinner?"

"Sounds wonderful." He said, getting out of the car.

We had a salad while Hawn curled up on her bed, worn out.

"I'll need to get her groomed tomorrow. There is a mobile groomer who'll come on Sunday. I'll book them. They might do it while I'm at my uncle and aunt's house in the morning."

"Tomorrow will be a clean-up day. My car and your dog." Mark grinned. "How about dinner tomorrow? We can finish the weekend as we started."

"I would love to, thanks."

"Okay, I better leave." He got up to go.

I walked him to the door. He put his arms around me and hugged me close. It felt great. I felt totally safe with him. Then he put his hand under my chin and kissed me, so gently and tenderly my legs went wobbly. I held on tightly to him to stop myself from collapsing.

"See you tomorrow." He whispered in my ear, and then he slipped out the door and closed it after him. I stood there for a few minutes, with my hand on the door, not trusting my legs to carry me back into the kitchen.

Before going to bed, I got online and booked the mobile groomer for the next morning at eleven, at Uncle Bill and Aunt Vickie's.

~~

It was just after ten when I got to their house. As usual, they were sitting out on the back patio. It was remarkably warm for April.

"Before I forget, the mobile groomer will be here at eleven to clean up Hawn. She's still shedding sand everywhere."

"Sand?" Uncle Bill said.

"Yeah. We spent the day at the beach yesterday. She loved it, but between swimming and then rolling in the sand, she was in a state. She made such a mess of Mark's car coming home."

"Mark? Your boss, Mark?" Aunt Vickie said, as she and Uncle Bill exchanged a concerned look.

"Yes." I smiled. "I think I need to bring him to meet you guys."

"So, it's getting serious?" Uncle Bill said.

"I hope so. Yes, it is. I know so. The more I get to know him, the more I like him. And more than that, I feel safe with him."

"How about you bring him to dinner on Friday?" Aunt Vickie said, giving Uncle Bill a stern look.

"I'll ask him and let you know."

My phone beeped to let me know the groomers had arrived. I brought Hawn around to the front and left her with them.

I spent the next two hours enjoying the time with my aunt and uncle while waiting for Hawn. They quizzed me on how work was going and if there was any news on the police search for Malcolm.

"I'm in regular contact with the police. They gave me a card in the hospital with a phone number I could call. So far nothing, but they are still searching. They promised to let me know as soon as they got any leads."

"How about Mark? Does the bank have any objection to staff fraternization?" Uncle Bill asked.

"Mark spoke to HR, and they said they have no problem, unless it interferes with our ability to get our work done. Their biggest concern was not that we were dating, but what would happen if we broke up?"

"Good point," Aunt Vickie said.

"Mark told them he would quit and find another job if they had a problem. They said they would prefer it if one, or both of us, requested a transfer, rather than quit. For now, we are just seeing where things go."

"But you do like him? And he's good to you?" I could tell Aunt Vickie was trying to sound casual, but she furrowed her brow as she asked.

"Yes, and yes. Please don't worry. I know I've made some dismal decisions, but I've never felt like this about anyone before in my life. I really do feel safe with him."

I didn't blame them for being worried. Naturally, I still didn't fully trust myself or my choices. But this time felt different. It was nothing like Malcolm, nor any of the dating site guys, least of all Sam. I really wanted this to work. Perhaps part of the difference was that I had gotten to know Mark as a person, a boss, a co-worker and a friend, before we started dating. Maybe that's what I was doing wrong before.

Just then, my phone beeped, letting me know Hawn was ready. They walked around the side of the house with me. Aunt Vickie wanted to see her all cleaned up. When they led Hawn out of the truck, Aunt Vickie and Uncle Bill made a fuss of her while I paid the groomers. Then we said goodbye, and I headed home with Hawn.

~~

By the time Mark arrived, at six-thirty, I'd prepared dinner, had a shower, and set the table. As it was Sunday evening, we agreed we should probably eat early.

Hawn made a tremendous fuss of Mark when he came in.

"You'd think she hadn't seen you in ages."

"She appreciates that I saved her from the stalker and brought her home. She definitely looks spruced up. So is my car." He grinned at her as he stroked her clean coat.

Over dinner, I asked him if he would be free on Friday.

"Aunt Vickie and Uncle Bill have invited us to dinner. And yes, before you ask, they plan to vet you carefully. I'm afraid they no longer trust my judgment."

"I can't fault them for that. And yes, I would love to meet them. What time?"

"Seven. Don't say I didn't warn you. They will interrogate you."

"And so they should. I don't have a problem with that."

After dinner, we cleared the table and then Mark put his arms around me and kissed me.

"I'm going home now. I don't want to, but it's Sunday night, and this week is going to be busy."

"I agree. I don't want you to go either. But, like you said, it's Sunday night."

He turned and gave Hawn a quick pat on the head. "Gotta go, Hawn, before I change my mind."

With that, he disappeared out the door.

As I locked up, I thought about how in tune we seemed to be. I'd been worried that he hoped to stay and that would not have been a good way to start the week. As he said, it was going to be a busy week. We'd a new teller and a loan officer starting.

CHAPTER THIRTY-TWO

I got into work extra early on Monday morning. As I was making the coffee, Mark came into the kitchen.

"Good morning, Sally," he said. "Did you have a good weekend?" He glanced around to make sure no one else was there before winking.

"Good morning, Mark." I matched his businesslike tone. "It was relatively quiet. Getting ready for a busy week."

He made a noise, something between a snort and a cough. Just then, Amanda came in. She stood beside him with her mug as he was pouring his own coffee. He filled her cup.

"Thanks Mark." She gave him a wide smile and looked like she was about to say something else when he turned and hurried out of the kitchen.

"What's wrong with him?"

"I imagine he has a lot to do. I know I do. Actually, you're going to be busy too, with training the new hire." I nodded to her and headed to my office.

The rest of the week flew past. I knew Mark was working late every evening. I didn't get to speak to him again until Friday morning. Once again, we were both in early, and were alone in the kitchen getting coffee.

"I'll pick you up at six-thirty, okay?" He whispered. "I'm going to wear khakis and a white shirt." He winked.

"Thanks for the warning. See you then." I whispered back, and we grinned at each other like school kids.

~~

By six-thirty, I had taken Hawn for a short walk. She would get to play in the yard later, so I wasn't too worried about that. I had a shower and had done my hair and makeup in record time. As I decided what to wear. I settled for comfort. Blue jeans and a light blue silk shirt. At least I knew this time we would not be in matching outfits.

Mark arrived at exactly six-thirty. When I opened the door, he stepped in and immediately wrapped me in his arms and kissed me.

"I've waited all week to do that." He said, kissing me again.

His car was spotlessly clean again. Fortunately, this time, so was Hawn. We pulled into Uncle Bill's front driveway, parking in almost the same spot that Malcolm's camper had been for so long. As I unloaded Hawn, Mark went to his trunk and lifted out an enormous bunch of flowers and a bottle of wine.

"Good move," I said, grinning at him. "Definite brownie points there."

The front door was already open, and Aunt Vickie came out to greet us. I could see Uncle Bill hovering in the hall, watching and waiting.

Introductions done, Aunt Vickie went into the house with the flowers to find a vase. We followed her. I introduced Mark to Uncle Bill. They shook hands, looking at each other, Uncle Bill with a stern stare and Mark with a hint of a smile.

"Delighted to meet you, sir," Mark said, handing over the bottle of wine.

"Good to meet you, too. Thanks for this." His face softened slightly. "Let's go try it. This way." He led the way into their massive formal dining room.

Aunt Vickie had gone all out. She had set the table with her best crystal glass, silver wear, and bone china. Uncle Bill opened the wine and poured us each a glass, as Aunt Vickie came in with the flowers and placed them on the sideboard, before taking her glass.

"Let's not waste time here, Mark. I'm sure Sally told you we're worried about her. After the horrible treatment she received from Malcolm, and not to mention being stalked by that other guy."

"I totally understand, sir. I would feel the same in your shoes. How about I give you my background? If you want to ask questions after that, I assure you, I'll answer them honestly."

We all sat down at the table with our glasses, and Mark recited his resume. He was thirty-two years old, born in Houston, Texas.

Attended Rice University. His parents were both dead. They had adopted him when they were already in their forties. He had never been married and had no children. He paused, waiting for questions.

"What brought you to this area?" Uncle Bill asked.

"I worked for the bank in Houston. When I was offered the manager position, it meant a transfer here."

Uncle Bill looked at him for a few seconds, then he smiled. "I think that covers all my questions. What about you, Vickie?"

"Really, Bill. This isn't a job interview." She looked at Mark. "Thank you for sharing that, Mark. How about we have dinner?"

Over dinner, Mark and Uncle Bill got into a conversation about sports and discovered they both followed the same football and baseball teams. And they both agreed to only having a mild interest in either sport. Mark refused a second glass of wine, saying he was driving. Uncle Bill nodded and smiled. Mark had passed another test, apparently. Aunt Vickie caught my eye and winked.

After dinner, we moved out to the patio where we had coffee and watched Hawn blow off some steam. As the light faded, we said our goodbyes. Mark thanked Aunt Vickie for a fantastic meal, and she hugged both of us. Uncle Bill walked us to the car and hugged me, then turned to Mark and shook hands with him.

"I look forward to doing this again. You must come to Sunday brunch with Sally. It's one of our traditions."

"Thank you, sir. I'll look forward to that."

~~

When we got to the apartment, Mark once again opened the trunk. This time, he lifted out a backpack. Carrying it over his shoulder, he followed me in.

"I believe we came to an agreement that I would be welcome to stay over." He said, raised eyebrows and slightly flushed cheeks, putting the backpack down in the hall.

I moved closer to him. "That was my understanding, too."

I could feel my face flush, and my heart fluttering as he put his arms around me. When he kissed me I felt like my entire body was blushing. Still kissing me, Mark started moving towards the kitchen. Finally, he stepped back.

"Let's go to bed." His voice was slightly husky.

I nodded, afraid to speak, not knowing if I still could. I settled Hawn for the night, took his hand and led him upstairs to the bedroom.

Next morning, I woke to the smell of bacon frying. As Mark was not in bed, I assumed he was downstairs cooking breakfast. I stretched and smiled to myself. I could get used to this. Putting on my robe, I went down to the kitchen. He smiled as I came in and he came over, handed me a mug of coffee, and kissed me.

"Breakfast will be ready soon. I found bacon and eggs in your fridge, so assumed that would be acceptable?"

"Wonderful, thank you."

~~

After breakfast, Mark suggested we drive over to his house. As we were getting ready to go, he asked me if we could bring Hawn along, too.

"I want to show both of you my home," He said, handing the leash to me.

He lived about twenty miles away, in a beautiful house with a huge backyard.

"Wow. This is impressive," I said.

"It was a dump when I bought it. I've spent the last five years renovating. I'm glad you like it."

He showed me around, and as we entered the kitchen, I spotted a dog bed, water dish and crate.

"I didn't know you had a dog!"

"I don't, but you do, and I want to make both of you feel welcome in my home. I got these last week, hoping you would spend some time here." He looked at me with his eyebrows raised.

"We'll certainly consider it," I said, not wanting to sound too eager and trying not to smile.

"Perhaps I can sell you on the backyard. It has a high fence and is pet friendly, and I can also install a doggie door to make Hawn comfortable."

"Now that sounds very tempting. That's something she's missing at the apartment."

Mark opened the back door and stepped out. Hawn was quivering and wagging her tail as she looked at me, waiting for permission to go.

As soon as I gave her the signal, she bounded out and immediately rolled around in the grass.

"See? She loves it."

"Okay. I give in." I said, trying to sound defeated, but I failed.

"Great! I'll have the doggie door fitted by next weekend."

The patio had a roof and a table with four cushioned chairs. We sat and watched as Hawn ran around sniffing every corner, flowerbed and tree more than once, before curling up on one of the chairs and going to sleep. Mark set about preparing lunch for us.

Later that afternoon, we headed back to my place. On the way, we stopped to pick up a takeout for dinner.

~~

Over the next few weeks, we slipped into a routine. I walked home as usual. What was not usual about my walk home every evening was now I kept a watch, not just for Sam, but also for Malcolm. Later, on Friday evenings, Mark came by, and we spent the weekend together. Most Friday nights, he stayed at the apartment. We drove to his place on Saturday mornings. He had fitted the doggie door, and Hawn had no difficulty using it.

On Sunday mornings, he came with me to Uncle Bill and Aunt Vickie's for brunch and, after dropping us back at my apartment, he went home.

We maintained a professional front at work, and no one had a clue that we were dating. I wasn't sure how long we could keep that to ourselves. Particularly as Amanda was still obviously flirting with Mark. She watched me closely whenever I was talking to him. Especially if he came into my office, which happened frequently, mostly for purely work-related meetings. I wondered why I ever thought it was a bad idea to date someone I worked with. I realized what matters is who that person is.

One Friday evening, after I got home, but before Mark arrived, my phone rang. It was the police officer who had talked to me in the hospital.

"Ms. Simms? Officer Johns here."

"Yes, this is Sally. Any news?" I held my breath.

"We had a report that someone saw that camper in Cambridge yesterday. We are checking it out and thought you would like to know.

If we've anything further, we'll let you know. But you might want to be extra vigilant."

"Thanks, I will for sure." My hands were shaking as I hung up.

CHAPTER THIRTY-THREE

One Saturday morning, as we were sitting down to have breakfast, my phone rang. As soon as I picked up, before I could say a word, a voice said.

"Don't hang up. I have some urgent information for you."

"Sam?" I said, looking at Mark, who had paused what he was doing to listen. I put it on speakerphone.

"Yes. Don't hang up." He repeated. "I was passing your place last night, and I saw your ex across the road—"

"You saw Malcolm? Here?"

"Yes, just listen. He was in the front yard of the house across the street from you. Behind a tree. You know? The house that's vacant? I'm going to send you a photo I took to prove it."

"You happened to be passing, and you were able to take a photo?"

My phone beeped, indicating a text. I tapped on the photo Sam had sent. Sure enough, it was Malcolm. The overgrown shrubbery partially hid him from view. He was standing behind a tree. As I zoomed in, it looked like he had a pair of binoculars in his hands.

"Okay, thanks Sam. But please stop stalking me. I've reported you to the police."

"What do you think?" I said, hanging up and handing the phone to Mark.

"No doubt about it. You've gained another stalker. You should call the police and send them that photo."

I took my phone back and pressed the contact number for the police.

"Hello, Officer Johns? This is Sally Simms again."

"Hi Sally. What can I do for you?"

"Someone called me this morning and said they saw Malcolm. He was watching my apartment from across the street."

"Can you be sure it was him?"

"They took a photo of him. I can send it to you if you'd like?"

"Please do."

I forwarded the photo to Officer Johns' phone number.

"Okay, just sent it via text."

"Thanks, we'll follow up."

I sat there looking at the phone for a few seconds. Not sure what to do next.

"Not much more you can do. The police will take care of it. Why don't you go have your shower and get dressed? I'll clear up here and we can take Hawn out for a walk. Perhaps we can spot him while we're out."

An hour later, we were ready to leave. As we walked out the front door, all hell broke loose. There was a loud bang. Mark fell and rolled down the steps onto the driveway, letting go of Hawn's leash. Hawn raced out and across the road, barking. And a police car pulled to a halt on the opposite side of the road.

I rushed down to where Mark lay still on the ground. There was blood all over his arm. I pulled off my sweatshirt and wrapped it around the wound in his arm, putting pressure on it as he opened his eyes.

"Sally. Are you hurt?" He said, trying to sit up.

"No. I'm fine, don't move. I'm going to call an ambulance."

Just as I was getting my phone out, two police officers came running into the yard, one of them leading Hawn.

"Here you go, Sally. I believe she's yours." Then he caught sight of Mark on the ground.

He immediately dropped on one knee beside him. He checked the wound, and talking into his radio, he called for an ambulance.

"Looks like the bullet went straight through. Just keep pressure on the wound and you should be okay." He looked up at me. "Your dog caught the shooter. He's in custody."

"It was Malcolm, wasn't it?" My voice came out in a squeak. I swallowed hard and repeated my question.

"Yes, it was."

I let out a long sigh and sat down on the ground beside Mark. I was shaking all over. He reached over to put an arm around me and let out a groan.

"Don't move, I'm okay. Just very relieved. Happy that you aren't seriously hurt and so glad that Malcolm's going to be locked up." I put my hand on his good arm. "I'm fine," I said as I stood up. I could hear the ambulance siren in the distance. I put Hawn back in the apartment so that I could go to the hospital with Mark.

When the ambulance arrived, the EMT checked Mark's wound. He bandaged it and loaded him into the back of the ambulance.

"I suggest you follow in your own car, miss. Looks like they might not need to admit him, seeing as the bullet went clean through."

The police had already dug it out of the front door.

As the ambulance headed off, I followed in my car. When I pulled out of the driveway, I spotted Malcolm being loaded into a squad car across the road.

~~

Four hours later, I drove Mark back to my place. We were lucky that the ER wasn't busy, and they saw him immediately.

They did all the usual stuff, filled him with various injections, and finally released him with his arm in a sling. The police had spoken with us at the hospital and had made an appointment for the following afternoon to get a full statement. They asked for contact information for Sam, so that they could speak to him too.

Mark insisted on coming with me to walk Hawn. This time, it was uneventful. We took her to the dog park and sat and watched her run around before walking back home.

"Luckily, I packed a bag for the weekend." He said as he sat watching me prepare dinner. "If I can't use this arm for a few days, driving would be difficult."

"Will you be okay to drive by tomorrow? If not, we'll need to get your work clothes from your place."

"We can wait and see."

We spent a quiet evening watching TV and went to bed early. It had been a very long and tiring day; despite Mark putting a brave face on it, he was very pale and I could see he was shaken.

On Sunday morning, we walked around to Uncle Bill and Aunt Vickie's for brunch. When they saw Mark's arm in a sling, naturally they wanted to know what happened to him.

"Oh, yeah. I probably should have called before we came, to let you know," I said.

"Turns out that Malcolm had been watching us and when he saw me at Sally's door, he shot me."

"He shot you!" Uncle Bill shouted.

"It's okay, Uncle Bill. The police got him. Well, actually Hawn got him, then the police saved him from her, and arrested him. We spent yesterday at the hospital. I'm afraid in the chaos I forgot to call you."

"Don't worry about that. But are you okay, son?" Uncle Bill said, his face creased with concern.

He had never addressed Malcolm as 'son'. Aunt Vickie stood beside him, speechless, gripping his good arm as though she was afraid he would fall.

"I'm fine, thanks. I have to admit it was a first. I've never been shot before and I hope it never happens again. I just kept thinking, thank goodness he shot me and not Sally."

They continued to make a fuss of him for the rest of the morning. Over our mimosas, we explained what had happened, glossing over the fact that we were coming out of the apartment first thing in the morning. They were more worried about how serious the wound was, and how much worse things could have been.

We left a little early in order to get back in time for the police statement.

After the police had left, I called Betty to tell her that Malcolm was under arrest. Of course, I had to rewind and explain to her from the beginning.

"Oh no! Is Mark okay? Are you okay? That's awful!"

"We are a bit shaken, I have to admit. It's very scary to think how much worse it could have been. Mark's still quite sore and can't drive for a few days, so he'll probably stay with me."

"Oh, please, can I be the one to tell Amanda?" she said.

"Tell her what?"

"That you're dating Mark, of course! Oh, I can't wait to see her face. She'll be livid."

I couldn't help laughing at her excitement.

"Well, just don't forget to tell your parents about Malcolm. They'll be glad to know he's going to pay for what he did to you."

We decided Mark should stay for the next week, or at least until he could drive safely. He had an appointment to have his wound checked the following Friday.

"Do you mind driving me home? I can pick up enough clothes to get me through the work week and we can decide on Friday what to do after that."

"Of course, I'll drive you. Let's go."

"Thank you for taking care of me." He leaned across and kissed me.

CHAPTER THIRTY-FOUR

Next morning, we left early. We wanted to be sure to get into work before anyone else, at least if they didn't see us arrive together, that would delay the inevitable. We were both seated in our respective offices, with our coffee mugs full, before anyone else got there.

The first to arrive was Betty. She came into my office bursting with excitement.

"Is Amanda here yet? Does she know? If not, can I tell her?"

I just shook my head and laughed.

"Why not just wait until she sees Mark's arm in a sling and asks what happened? Then you can casually say something like 'Oh, didn't you hear? He spent the night with Sally. Malcolm got jealous and shot him.' Then watch the fireworks."

We both giggled, then snorted as we tried to suppress the sound, making it worse. It was more hysteria than amusement on my part. I was still trying to make sense of the fact that Mark had been shot and could have been killed. I didn't want to even think about that.

"I better get back to my desk in case Amanda comes in. Certainly don't want to miss this." Betty was still giggling when she left my office.

What actually happened was even funnier. Mark didn't emerge from his office all morning, but at lunchtime, a group of us were milling around the kitchen when he came in with his empty coffee mug.

"Oh, my goodness Mark! What happened to your arm?" Amanda said.

I saw Betty open her mouth, but before she could say a word, Mark put his coffee cup on the table and put his arm around me.

"I was coming out of Sally's place early on Saturday morning.

Malcolm was hiding across the road. I guess he was jealous, and he shot me. Luckily, it was an ordinary rifle and not an AR15. Don't worry, though, Hawn detained him, and the police arrested him." He gave me a hug, picked up the coffeepot, refilled his mug, and walked back to his office. All with a straight face.

Betty choked and coughed. I patted her on the back.

"Are you okay?"

She nodded, still coughing. She headed to the restroom. I grabbed my lunch and my coffee and hurried to my office before Amanda recovered from the shock. She was standing in the middle of the kitchen, her mouth opening and closing, making no sound. I hadn't expected Mark to do that, but it was definitely hilarious.

Amanda spent the rest of the day scowling across the floor at my office.

~~

As we walked home that evening, I asked Mark why he had said what he did.

"I don't know. I've wanted to put her in her place for so long, I couldn't resist the opportunity." He chuckled. "It was worth it to see the look on her face."

"It was hilarious. Betty had planned to say something similar, but she was too slow. But far better coming from you."

That evening, the police officer who arrested Malcolm informed me they had arraigned him, and that the judge had refused bail because he considered him a flight risk. I noted down the dates he gave me. The first, an appointment to speak with the prosecutor, both for myself and for Mark. Betty would also be called in. And the second, the date set for the trial. We would need to make ourselves available, should those dates change.

The rest of the week went smoothly until Friday. Mark drove us to work on Friday morning. He planned to head to the hospital and then to his own house after work and drove in to be sure he was comfortable driving, before he tried the longer trip.

At ten, two guys from the head office came into the bank and asked to see Mark. After about thirty minutes, they came out and Mark led them to one of the conference rooms. Then he came into my office and closed the door.

"What's up?" I asked as he sat down opposite me.

"Head office." He nodded towards the conference room. "They received a complaint about 'fraternization' between staff members. Apparently, someone finds it distressing and interfering with their ability to do their job."

"And they didn't tell you her name?" I said.

"No. They didn't need to. I am certain it was Amanda."

"So, what are they going to do about it? They know you already spoke to HR, right?"

He nodded. "They're going to interview all the staff and then decide."

"I guess we better be ready to polish up our resumes?"

"Not yet. It sounded like they felt this was a massive waste of their time. Let's wait and see."

For the rest of the morning and most of the afternoon, I watched as one person after another disappeared into the conference room, returning to their desks after about twenty minutes.

As soon as Betty finished with them, she came into my office with a handful of papers, trying to look like she was talking about business.

"They asked a bunch of questions about the atmosphere here. Then they said, on no account should I talk to anyone else about what they had asked me."

"But you just did!"

"Well, no. I didn't tell you the actual questions. And I didn't tell anyone else. I doubt they meant you, because they aren't going to interview you. They just didn't want the rest of the staff to be forewarned."

"To my knowledge, everyone—except Amanda—is very happy here."

"I agree, and I told them that. They said they would let us all know before the end of the day what their decision is."

"Thanks Betty," I said, as she gathered up her papers and went back to her desk.

The last person to be interviewed was Amanda. She was in there for at least forty-five minutes. When she came out, she went back to her station, shut everything down and left the building. Shortly after that, the two men came out and spent another thirty minutes in Mark's office before returning to the conference room.

As soon as security closed the doors to the public, Mark came out and announced that there was an all-staff meeting. Everyone gathered on the floor, waiting and whispering to each other. There was a sudden silence as the conference room door opened.

One man went over and stood beside Mark, while the other looked around to see if he had everyone's attention. Hardly necessary.

"Thank you all for putting up with this disruption to your day." He cleared his throat before continuing. "I'll report back to head office that this is a very happy, well-run branch. We thank you for your good work and wish you all a very good evening." They both nodded to Mark and left.

Mark clapped his hands to quiet the sudden clamoring of conversation.

"I have a couple of things to say." He waited until he had everyone's full attention. "First, thank you all very much. I understand you had many nice things to say about me, and about Sally, as your manager and assistant manager. Second, Amanda has accepted a transfer to the Boston branch effective immediately."

There was some clapping and laughing before everyone started talking again. Mark took my elbow and drew me into his office, closing the door.

As he sat down behind his desk, he had a huge grin on his face.

"What?" I said.

"Apparently Amanda has been inundating head office for weeks, with complaints of all sorts. She didn't get the AM position; someone who only just joined the bank, someone she trained got it. Lots of other irrelevant stuff. They were trying to decide what to do about her when she made the complaint about us."

"So, this whole day was a pretense?"

"No, they had to have a record of following up on her complaint, and make sure she was the only one who was unhappy. But they had already identified a position in Boston. They offered her a choice: take that position or leave."

"Poor girl," I said. "She's her own worst enemy, and goodness knows, nobody here likes her either." I couldn't help feeling sorry for her.

"Anyway. At least we don't have to go through the motions, pretending we're not a couple anymore. Not only is Amanda gone, but everyone knows and supports us."

CHAPTER THIRTY-FIVE

Later that Friday evening, I got a call from Ted.

"Sally? Hey, it's Ted. Not sure if you remember me? We exchanged Grace in White Plains over a year ago. You kindly delivered her to Bangor?"

"Hi Ted, of course I remember you! How are you?"

"I'm doing great, thanks. I moved back to Austin. Pat and I are running the Escape Route for Caitlin. We have another client who needs transportation from Hartford, Connecticut, to Boston. I was hoping you could do it?"

"I would be delighted to help. When?"

"Tomorrow, if that's possible?"

"Saturday? No problem at all."

"Great, let me give you the address where you'll pick up Elizabeth and where she's to be dropped off."

Ted gave me the details and as soon as I hung up, I turned to Mark, who'd been listening.

"That's the Escape Route that helped me to get away from Malcolm—the first time. I have to help."

"Of course you do. Hartford is less than three hours away. You can easily do that round trip in a day. Anything I can do to help?"

"Just the fact that you support me is help enough. Though I would appreciate it if you could take care of Hawn for the day?"

"No problem. I'll bring her over to my place in the morning, and you can join us there when you get back."

"Perfect. Thanks."

~~

Next morning, I was on the road at eight. I expected to pick up Elizabeth at approximately eleven and be back on the road to Boston by one at the latest, allowing for lunch and a brief rest. The drive was longer than the last one, to New Haven, but not nearly as long as the one I had done to White Plains.

The trip out was uneventful. It took less than two and a half hours, which was lucky, because I got a bit lost as I drove into Hartford. Thanks to the GPS, I found the address. The woman who answered my knock looked like she was in her fifties. She introduced herself as Mabel and invited me in, leading me to the kitchen where they were having coffee. Elizabeth was about my age, with long dark hair. It didn't surprise me to see she had a black eye and bruised face, though it did anger me. Mable explained she had collected her from Philly the day before.

"I would have been prepared to drive her on to Boston this morning if you had not been available. We appreciate your help."

"Of course. I'm happy to do it."

"I'm about to make some sandwiches. Not too early for lunch, I hope?"

"No, indeed. I was on the road early and would appreciate a snack and a chance to relax before heading off again."

I looked at Elizabeth. So far, she hadn't said a word.

"How are you feeling, Elizabeth?"

"Stupid," she said, looking down at her empty mug.

"Don't. Seriously. I don't know about Mabel, but I've been in your seat. Almost two years ago. Caitlin helped me to escape from Austin. You have nothing to be embarrassed about, certainly not with me. I know exactly what you have been through and what you are feeling now. Just be happy you found Caitlin's Escape Route. Feel lucky, not stupid."

"Well said Sally," Mabel said. "Me too."

Elizabeth smiled. "Call me Liz. And thank you both. Thank you very much."

By one we were back on the road, heading towards Boston.

"Have you family in Boston?" I asked as we set off.

"My brother lives there. I'll stay with him for a few days and then we are going to drive to Portland, Maine. That's where my parents live, where I grew up."

"We're so lucky to have family to return to."

She nodded, saying nothing.

"I understand if you would like me to keep quiet. I'm also happy to listen or to talk. Up to you."

She smiled. "Actually, I would love to hear your story. Like I said, I feel so very stupid. It helps to know I'm not the only one."

Although it was not something I like to even think about anymore. I was very aware of how much it helped me to know what Pat had gone through. It made me feel less embarrassed. So, as we drove, I told Liz my story.

I explained how I'd met Malcolm, the beatings; how they got worse each time. I told her how I'd met Caitlin in a restaurant one evening when he was in a particularly bad humor, and she had noticed. That was when she gave me her contact details in the restroom. I saw her go into her house as we were driving past on our way home. How I'd run to her when he attacked me that evening and she'd immediately opened her door and the Escape Route to me.

"What I'm most embarrassed about is the fact that Malcolm tracked me down, and I took him back."

"No! What happened then?"

"He swore that he'd taken anger management and was a changed person. I got pregnant. He hadn't changed, and he got abusive again. When I told him to leave, he beat me so badly I lost the baby."

We were both silent for a few minutes.

"I had a miscarriage too. Last month. After Don beat me. But I went back to him, when I got out of the hospital. He accused me of having an abortion. Then he beat me again. That was when I left. I won't ever take him back again."

"Good for you! We deserve better."

"Thank you for telling me your story. It makes me feel a lot better."

"I wonder, does Caitlin know we supply therapy as we drive?" I said, laughing. "By the way, I recommend you go for therapy once you get settled. I guarantee you it helps a bunch."

"Okay. Pat said that to me before I left Austin. I didn't get to meet Caitlin."

"Yeah, Pat was my driver on my first leg out of Austin. I heard she's now helping to run the Escape Route. They're amazing people."

"So are you. And when I get settled, I'll try to help any way I can, too," Liz said.

We drove the rest of the way in silence, each of us lost in our own thoughts.

Sometime later, I dropped her off at her brother's apartment on the outskirts of Boston, wished her good luck and called Mabel to report that I had safely delivered her. Then I headed to Mark's.

It was approaching five when I finally pulled into the driveway. Mark and Hawn came out to greet me. As Hawn waited patiently for attention, I hugged Mark extra tight. Then bent down and hugged her too.

"Come on, I bet you could use a drink." Mark led me into the house.

CHAPTER THIRTY-SIX

The following month was a series of meetings with Allen, a member of the prosecution team, Betty and her father, Paul. It meant we had to take time off work, but while it was a problem for us, as we had to work late to catch up, it was not a problem for the bank. As victims, we had a right and a duty to cooperate, and they fully supported us.

We were told that Sam was also a witness for the prosecution and had spoken to them at length. Fortunately, not at the same time as us.

"I've rarely found a stalker to be so useful," Allen said. "He's a very peculiar guy. He seems to believe that he's doing a service to the community by his behavior. To be fair, this time I guess he did. But he doesn't understand that stalking is creepy and wrong."

"Yeah, during the short time I was dating him, he was also stalking his ex-girlfriend. He felt justified, was even proud of himself. That's why we split up."

"The photographs he took are crucial evidence. He seemed to think that justified what he had done." Allen shook his head before continuing to work through his list of questions.

"Okay." He finally stood up. "I think I have all the information I need. I'll start working on my presentation. Let's meet again in a week. We can do a trial prep."

"A trial prep?" Mark said.

"Yes. I'll walk you through the questions I intend to ask at trial, and also the questions the defense is likely to ask you on cross examination."

"Ah, okay. Sounds good."

"We'll go over that a few times before the trial. The idea is to avoid any major surprises. It's not always possible, but we'll do our best."

He walked with us to the exit. "Thanks for coming in. See you next week."

Although it was late afternoon, we went back to the bank and worked for a few hours, clearing our desks for the next day.

We repeated the process the following week, except that was a very much longer and more stressful experience.

Allen led us down to an empty courtroom. We each had to sit in the witness box and answer his question from there. The prosecution's questions were not nearly as difficult to deal with as the questions he had assumed the defense might ask.

"One of the questions I'm going to ask you is one that the defense will not be happy about. I need to introduce the fact that he has a history of being violent. So, I'll ask you why you took him back when he had done this to you before."

I nodded, feeling embarrassed. "Okay, he said he had done anger management, and I wanted to believe it had worked. I wanted to give him the benefit of the doubt." Glancing at Mark. I could feel myself blush. "I know it was stupid of me, but—"

"Okay, that's good. Just be prepared for the defense to try to make you look like the guilty party. I've no doubt he'll try to claim self-defense."

By the time he had finished with us, we were exhausted.

"Let's go take care of Hawn and go get something to eat. We can go into work early tomorrow and see to anything that needs our attention then," Mark said.

"Good idea. You can stay over at my place tonight." Mark now kept a few items of clothes at my apartment for just such occasions. I did the same at his place. "I'll be glad when this trial is over. Not just because I can't relax until I know we're safe from Malcolm, but this practicing is no fun."

Mark nodded. "Just one more prep session and we'll be ready. And it'll be worth it."

I had to agree with him there.

"I'm so very sorry, Mark."

"Sorry for what?"

"For being stupid enough to believe that Malcolm could change, and for causing all of this."

Sally's Story

"Malcolm caused this. You didn't."

~~

The day before the trial was due to start, we got a call from Allen. Well, Mark got the call. We were at work, and he came into my office to tell me.

"Allen just called me. He said to tell you Malcolm has settled for a plea deal."

"Seriously? So, no trial?"

"That's right. Apparently, according to Allen, his defense lawyer convinced him he didn't have a chance of getting off. Sam's photos sealed it. Some of them showed him with a rifle, and the location was obvious from the house in the background."

"But he is going to prison, right?"

"Oh yeah. He's to plead guilty to all three charges. Shooting me, attacking Betty, and attacking you, plus losing the baby. With his existing record, Allen thinks he'll get at least five years."

I felt the tension drain out of my body. Tension I had not realized was there.

"I wonder, does Betty know?"

"No doubt they have called her lawyer, but we might as well tell her."

Mark stuck his head out of my office and called her. She came in, and when he told her, she let out a squeal and then sat down suddenly on the chair by my desk.

"My parents will be so happy!" she said. "Oh, what a relief." She got up and almost ran back to her desk to call her dad.

Mark grinned at me. "You should probably call Bill and Vickie too. They were planning to be at the trial."

"Good point. I'll do that now."

~~

That Sunday, brunch was even more cheerful than usual. Uncle Bill and Aunt Vickie were thrilled that it had finally ended.

"What are you going to do now?" Aunt Vickie asked me.

"Live. I feel as though my life has been on hold for months. It's time to relax and enjoy the last of the summer." I raised my glass, and they all raised theirs.

"I've a surprise." Mark said. "I was going to do this when the trial finished, but as soon as Allen called, I put my plan into action."

"What?" I said.

"I have booked a week's vacation for both of us, starting next week. We're flying to Austin. You can visit your friends there." He looked at Uncle Bill. "I'm hoping that Bill and Vickie can take care of Hawn for you?"

"Absolutely! We would be delighted to. A vacation is exactly what both of you need, after all you have gone through."

I jumped up and hugged Mark.

"Oh, how lovely! I can't think of anywhere I would rather go. Thank you! I can't remember the last time I had a vacation."

I pulled out my phone and started working on a list. People in Austin to contact, things to pack, stuff to finish up at work.

"Another list?" Aunt Vickie said, smiling.

CHAPTER THIRTY-SEVEN

We had an early morning flight out of Boston. The sky was clear and as we took off, I could see the city spread below. The coastline and, in the distance, the forests. They were showing the full signs of fall colors. It was beautiful and felt like home to me. Although both Mark and I grew up in Texas, we both felt that New England was where we belonged, and more specifically, in Cambridge.

As we approached Austin airport, however, I felt almost the same. This was home. The heat shimmering off the dried-up countryside, the winding Colorado River, and the series of lakes. It was two years since I left, beaten and miserable. How much had changed. How very lucky I was. Mark squeezed my hand, and I looked up at him.

"Home again."

I nodded and sighed. It was a happy sigh.

Before we left Cambridge, I'd called Pat to let her know I would be in Austin and hoped to see her. She was thrilled and two days later she called me back to say that Caitlin suggested we use one of the units next to her as it was currently vacant, if we needed somewhere to stay.

When I ran to Caitlin for help, she was living in a duplex. Apparently, after that she had purchased a fourplex and while she occupied one unit, Pat and Ted also had one each. And they rented one out. It turned out that Pat and Ted were now living together, and Caitlin had bought a house on the lake after she got married. The other units were rented out, but one was still vacant. We accepted. Not only would it save money on accommodation, but it also meant we could spend more time with all of Caitlin's Escape Route people.

We picked up a car at the airport. It felt surreal to drive through familiar streets, past familiar buildings. We even passed the bank where

I had worked with Malcolm. As we pulled into the driveway shared by all four of the units, the end unit door opened, and Pat and Ted came running towards the car. I got out and hugged both of them, then introduced them to Mark.

"Let me show you your unit." Ted said, leading us to one of the center units. "It's been empty for a while, but we had it cleaned yesterday. You should be comfortable."

"Thank you. We really appreciate it." Mark said.

"I stocked the kitchen with the essentials. There's a convenience store around the corner if you need anything else," Pat said.

"You are so good, thank you." I smiled at her.

"After all the help you have given us, it's very little."

"After all the help you gave me, I still owe you so much," I said.

"We'll let you get settled in. Then dinner tonight?"

"Sounds wonderful. Thanks."

"Oh, and Caitlin and George have invited us all over to their place for dinner tomorrow. Wait till you see it. It's gorgeous, right on the lake."

That evening, we had dinner with Ted and Pat. The restaurant was within walking distance, so we shared a bottle of wine, as no one was driving. Walking home in that Texas heat reminded me of one of the things I loved about New England. Apart from the beautiful fall colors, the changing seasons were a relief from the heat that was almost constant in Texas for most of the year.

~~

The following day, we had a lazy day planned. Apart from a visit to the bank where I used to work, we just sat out on the back patio and relaxed.

In the evening, Ted drove us all out to Caitlin's house for dinner. I only barely remember what Caitlin looked like. The first and only time I met her was just before and immediately after Malcolm had badly beaten me. I was probably in shock, definitely in pain and no question, I was mortally embarrassed. She greeted me like a long-lost friend.

"Sally! It's so good to see you. I rarely get to meet my clients once they head into the ER. This is exciting."

Ted took care of the introductions all around and then they led us out to the patio. It was a Spanish-style house with balconies and large windows. It stood on the side of a steep cliff overlooking the lake.

"What a beautiful place," I said, sitting down.

Caitlin smiled. "It took us ages to find it. I love it here. Terri, my sister, lives further up the lake. She and her husband will join us." She stood up. "In fact, that's them now."

Terri didn't look at all like Caitlin. Caitlin was not much over five feet tall, with dark auburn hair. Terri was almost as tall as me and had blonde hair.

It was an amazing meal. Caitlin and Terri regaled us with stories from their childhood growing up on the West Coast of Ireland. How they came up with the idea of the Escape Route, after Terri had been beaten and locked in her home, which her abuser, her husband at the time, set fire to.

"He was arrested, tried, and convicted. He escaped from the police, while on the way to serve his sentence," Terri said, staring out over the lake. Her husband, Joe, squeezed her hand.

"Sorry." She smiled. "That was over a year ago now."

"Did they catch him?" Mark asked.

"He was stupid enough to come back here. He kidnapped Terri and held her for ransom," George said.

"No!" I couldn't believe it.

"Yes, we rescued her, but he was not so lucky. Apparently, he'd become involved with some drug smugglers in Mexico and double crossed them. They shot him."

"So, everyone here has been a victim of some form of domestic violence? Except Mark?"

"And me." Joe said. "It would appear we are the exception." He nodded to Mark.

"Well, thank goodness for you, Caitlin," Mark said.

"So, Sally, tell us what you have been doing since you escaped. Clearly, you recovered and are now in a good relationship," Caitlin said, smiling at Mark. "Not only that, I understand that you have also helped our efforts more than once."

"I'm sorry to say I let you down," I said.

I told them how Malcolm had tracked me down and I had given in and taken him back.

"He assured me he'd attended anger management, and I trusted he had changed. He hadn't."

"It would surprise you how often that happens. I know of cases where anger management does work, but they're rare," Caitlin said. "But don't blame yourself. Clearly, it was something you had to do in order to finally get past it. And you did."

"That was the same guy you kicked down the stairs, wasn't it?" George, Caitlin's husband asked her.

She blushed. "He was coming up the stairs to attack me. I kicked him and he fell down the stairs."

"No! He was going to attack you?" I said.

"He wanted to know where you were."

"You kicked him?" Mark said, looking surprised.

George grinned. "I didn't know it then, but this little woman is an expert in more than one martial art."

Everyone looked at her in silence for a few seconds.

"Wow," I said. "I wish I could have seen that!"

"I saw her floor my ex-husband. She saved my life and handed him over to the police," Terri said. "It was scary when it happened, but fun to think about now."

The sunset was beautiful over the lake and, as the sky darkened, we said goodbye.

"Thank you for a wonderful meal and for saving my life," I said to Caitlin as we left.

"You are very welcome. Thank you for visiting. It's wonderful to know that what we're doing makes a difference. Come back anytime."

The rest of our week was uneventful. We did some of the tourist things, such as the Bob Bullock Museum, and took a trip to San Antonio to visit the Alamo and the River Walk. Although Mark had grown up in Houston, he had rarely visited Austin and had never been to any of these places. We flew home on Saturday afternoon.

As I watched the city below me, and the lakes in the distance, I decided that, yes; I loved Austin. It's where I grew up. But Cambridge was my home. Mark was relieved. He told me he'd planned the trip so that I could decide if I wanted to return to Texas or stay in Massachusetts.

We were going to pick up Hawn from Uncle Bill and Aunt Vickie the following day. I was looking forward to seeing them.

CHAPTER THIRTY-EIGHT

Mark seemed to enjoy our Sunday brunch visits as much as I did. He and Uncle Bill became firm friends. They had a lot in common, apart from sports teams. They read the same books and had the same political views.

Aunt Vickie and I got used to them getting deep into conversations, and we ignored them most of the time. One Sunday, although it was cold outside, they went out into the backyard and started walking around, stopping occasionally. On the way home, I asked Mark what they were talking about.

"I wanted his opinion on what trees to plant. He was giving me a rundown on his favorites."

I thought it was strange but forgot about it until the following Friday evening.

~~

As usual, after work, I walked home. Mark always worked later than everyone else. It gave me time to take Hawn for a walk and prepare dinner. When I got home, it surprised me to see Mark's car already outside. I hadn't noticed him leaving the bank before I did. I knew he would be inside preparing dinner.

As I walked into the kitchen, the sight was definitely not what I expected. There were vases of roses all over the place. A bottle of unopened champagne sat on the table with two delicate crystal flute glasses. And in the middle of all that, Mark, on one knee, holding out a small box to me.

"Sally, will you marry me?"

I sank to my knees in front of him, blinking back tears. I opened and closed my mouth twice; no sound came out.

"Please?" Mark looked worried.

I swallowed and tried again. "Yes." It came out as a squeak. "Yes, please." I said more clearly and threw my arms around him. He lost his balance, and we landed in a heap on the ground. Hawn decided we were playing and joined us. As we untangled ourselves and stood up, Mark placed the box in my hand.

I stared at it, speechless. Sitting on the white satin pillow was a beautiful antique diamond solitaire ring.

"It was my great-grandmother's. It was passed down from her to my mother. Now it's yours. We can get it sized if it doesn't fit." He said as he slipped it on my finger.

I could no longer control the tears. Hawn sat at my feet, whining at me, worried.

I kneeled down and hugged her. "It's okay, Hawn. They're happy tears this time." I felt like I was in a dream. If Malcolm hadn't tried to get rid of Hawn, I would never have allowed myself to get close to Mark.

"I can't believe how much I love you." I reached up and kissed him.

"I think I fell in love with you that very first day, when I interviewed you." He replied.

"Oh. I have to tell Uncle Bill and Aunt Vickie!" I pulled my phone out of my purse.

Mark just smiled as he opened the bottle of champagne.

"Aunt Vickie?" I said as soon as she picked up. "Put me on speakerphone. I've something to tell you both."

"Go ahead." I heard Uncle Bill say.

"Mark proposed!"

"And I hope you accepted?" Uncle Bill said.

"Yes, yes, I did. You don't sound very surprised?"

"He asked my permission. Last Sunday when we were discussing trees." Uncle Bill and Aunt Vickie both laughed.

"Oh." I looked at Mark. "I presume you said yes, like I did."

"I did. And your Aunt Vickie's already looking at wedding venues and stuff like that."

"Wait till you see the ring. I'll show it to you on Sunday."

I said goodbye and hung up as Mark handed me a glass of champagne.

Over dinner, we talked about our future.

"I would like you to think about moving in with me," Mark said. "I know you want to be close to your aunt and uncle, but it makes more sense. My place is more than big enough and gives Hawn more space."

"I agree. It makes sense. My lease is coming up for renewal next month. It would be nice not to have to pay rent. I could pay off Uncle Bill much faster for all his help."

"So, that's another yes?"

"Yes."

As Mark refilled my glass, I had a sudden thought.

"Oh! Will we have to tell them at work? I guess I could just not wear my ring during the week. Thank goodness Amanda's gone. She would go ape shit!" The thought of how she would react, and possibly the champagne, gave me a fit of giggles.

Mark grinned. "No. Wear your ring. Let's see how long it takes someone to notice."

I glanced down at my hand. "It's beautiful. I would hate to not wear it. I'm so glad that it fits, so I don't have to part with it to be sized."

"I'm relieved you like it. Some women prefer to select their own ring, I hear. I asked Bill if perhaps you had your mother's ring."

"She never had an engagement ring. I have her wedding ring. But I wear that on a chain around my neck."

~~

I'd spent the week going through my closet every evening. Packed everything I didn't need immediately and put aside clothes to donate. We spent Saturday identifying the few items I wanted to keep. The rest were being picked up first thing in the morning by the local church.

Neither Mark nor I were religious, but Betty's mom had put us in touch with her church group, and they were delighted to take anything I was prepared to give. They had several needy families to whom they would deliver.

The stuff I was keeping, and my clothes would easily fit in both cars. The only thing left to do was to transport Hawn's crate and bed to Uncle Bill and Aunt Vickie, for when they would be called on to take care of her. We certainly didn't need two. Our plan was to bring those over when we went for Sunday brunch. Then, in the afternoon, we would load up the cars with everything else and head over to Mark's house.

I had allocated the following weekend to cleaning up the apartment and handing over the keys.

I had expected to feel strange once I was officially living with Mark. But it felt normal. Partly because we had spent almost every weekend together since I got Hawn back. But also in part, because it felt so very right.

It wasn't my house, but it was my home. I hadn't been involved in choosing furniture, fittings, or colors for the walls. Any of that. But it was all exactly as I would have chosen. I wouldn't change any of it.

By the end of the first week, I had identified a dog park and several routes to walk to it. Mark's local shops were actually much better than mine, besides living there didn't limit us to shopping there.

~~

On Friday evening, Uncle Bill and Aunt Vickie came to dinner. I wanted them to see my new home, and I know they were very keen to satisfy themselves that I was comfortable. As we showed them around the house, I could tell it impressed them.

"And you did all this renovation yourself?" Aunt Vickie said more than once.

"Beautiful home." Uncle Bill said as we settled ourselves in the chairs on the patio.

Mark was grilling steaks, and I had already made a salad. There was nothing for me to do but relax and enjoy the company.

~~

The following day, I stood in the empty apartment and thought about the events of the past two, almost three years—since I first moved in with Malcolm, in Austin. Back then, I was so sure I had found my soul mate. Now I knew I had. So where did I go wrong? Was I wrong again? Then I remembered a question my therapist had asked me.

"Do you think you're trying to recreate your parents' relationship?"

I thought it was a weird thing to ask. And it made little sense. I said, of course, I wanted to have a relationship like theirs; in my memory it was perfect. But was I trying to recreate it? I didn't think so. Now the question made sense. I think that's exactly what I was trying to do. With Malcolm, with the dating app and Sam, and a second time with Malcolm, though, I should have known that wouldn't work.

This time, I hadn't even considered Mark as a candidate for my future happiness. That just happened.

Finally, I understood what Rick was getting at. I was so determined to have a relationship like my parents' that I compromised everything to make it work. I missed the fact that both parties have to be equally committed. In my determination to recreate my parents' relationship, I was blind to Malcolm's faults.

I looked forward to my next appointment with Rick so I could tell him. I was still seeing him once a month. Perhaps it was finally time to tell him goodbye.

THE ESCAPE ROUTE SERIES

Book 1: Caitlin's Escape Route

Book 2: Sally's Story

Book 3: Coming Soon

ABOUT THE AUTHOR

Aideen was born in Dublin, Ireland. In 1994 she emigrated to America, having won a green card in the lottery. She now lives just outside Austin, Texas.
She worked as a Software Quality Assurance Engineering Manager until her retirement in May 2021.
Her first book, Peeling The Onion, a memoir, was published in 2013. Sally's Story is the second novel in The Escape Route Series.
When she is not writing, she enjoys fishing or boating on Lake Travis.

Printed in Great Britain
by Amazon